# Falling

## *to*

# Pieces

A ROSE GARDNER

BETWEEN THE NUMBERS NOVELLA

THIRTY AND THIRTY-ONE

# Other books by Denise Grover Swank:

# Falling

*to*

# Pieces

A ROSE GARDNER
BETWEEN THE NUMBERS NOVELLA

THIRTY AND THIRTY-ONE

## Denise Grover Swank

This book is a work of fiction. References to real people, events, establishments, organizations, or locations are intended only to provide a sense of authenticity, and are used factiously. All other characters, and all incidents and dialogue, are drawn from the author's imagination and are not to be construed as real.

# Part One

## Rose

# Chapter One

Joe stood in my front door, his voice breaking. "Goodbye, Rose." Then the door shut behind him.

The unthinkable just happened. Joe left me.

My lungs burned for air, but my body had forgotten how to breathe. As though Joe had sucked all the air from my house with him when he told me it was over.

My vision fogged, and a huge lump filled my throat, but I still couldn't take a breath. I fell to my hands and knees. The door was blurry through the tears that filled my eyes but refused to fall. It was like every part of me forgot how to function. As if Joe had announced we were done, stuck a pin in me, and left me a collapsed heap on the floor. There was nothing left of me now but skin and bones and a shattered heart.

*Just breathe.*

Breathing was the most natural thing in the world, but nothing in a world without Joe was natural. I'd heard of people who died from broken hearts, but I realized that wasn't necessarily true. They died because their bodies forgot how to live.

The room grew darker as I was closer to passing out. Finally, my body found the will I couldn't summon, and I sucked in a breath, releasing it with a sob.

This wasn't happening.

I lay on the floor for what could have been minutes, or hours or even days, sobbing so long there shouldn't be tears left, yet the bottomless well of despair remained.

"Rose?" Neely Kate's worried voice came from my front door.

I lifted my head off the floor to see her shocked face. She hurried over and knelt beside me. "Rose, what happened?" Her words were strangled.

I tried to catch my breath. "He...e's gone."

"Who's gone?"

"Joe."

She shook her head, tears in her eyes. "Rose, I don't understand. He just called me. He sounded upset and told me you needed me...oh." Her voice faded. "*What happened?*"

How did I explain that the only man I'd ever loved left me to protect me?

Neely Kate grabbed my arms and pulled me to a sitting position, worry in her eyes. "You need to calm down, sweetie. You're all banged up from last night. All this cryin' can't be any good for your head."

What did it matter?

"Come on. Let's at least get you on the sofa, okay?"

I let her help me up off the floor and settle me on the cushions while I tried to get control of my crying. I heard her voice while she talked on her phone, the last ten minutes with Joe replaying in my head. When had it all gone wrong?

The next thing I knew, Violet was kneeling in front of me, looking up into my face. "Rose, what happened?"

I opened my mouth to answer but nothing came out. Neely Kate handed me a glass of ice water, and I took a sip.

"Did you guys have a fight?" Neely Kate asked.

"No." My voice sounded hoarse from all my crying.

"I don't understand why you're so upset. What happened?" Violet sat next to me and squeezed my hand.

"Joe broke up with me this morning."

Neely Kate sat on the floor in front of me, shaking her head. "That doesn't make one lick of sense. He's crazy about you."

What was I going to tell them? I couldn't tell them the truth. I had to protect Violet. "He's decided to run for the state senate. His family doesn't find me acceptable."

Violet lifted my hand, staring at the ring still on my finger. "Then why are you wearing an engagement ring?"

I closed my eyes and leaned back into the cushions. "He proposed last night." I swallowed, my fuzzy mind trying to piece together a story they would believe. "I went to dinner at his parents' house—"

"You didn't tell me you were going to meet his parents," Neely Kate said.

My chin trembled. "It all happened so fast. Joe called and asked me to come at the last minute. But it was a disaster. There were about twenty people all dressed up in tuxedos and long dresses and I... wasn't. His parents didn't approve of me, and I didn't fit in with their friends." I looked into Neely Kate's eyes. "And Hilary was there."

They both gasped.

"Why was *she* there?" Violet's tone was cold, and it was nice to hear her using it on someone other than me.

I thought about the vision I had of Joe with a pregnant Hilary and swallowed the tears threatening to resurface. "Her family is close to Joe's. She'll *always* be there." I sighed with resignation.

"But he *proposed* to you. Why would he break up?" Neely Kate asked.

"His father announced that Joe's running for the state senate. And everyone was so awful at dinner." I shook my head. "It was clear to all of us I didn't belong there."

Violet tugged on my hand. "Rose, this is crazy. Joe *loves* you. There's no way he'd just dump you to run for the state senate."

I looked out the window into the side yard. I wanted to tell her the truth, but I couldn't do it with Neely Kate there. Not after Violet confessed the night before that she'd had an affair while she was still living with Mike, and that Mike suspected and threatened to take the kids from her if he found out it was true. If Joe's family released the photos they had of Violet and Brody, Henryetta's married mayor, she would be destroyed. She may have been awful to me the last few months, but she was still my sister. She'd been there for me for twenty-four years. That had to overshadow a few months of jealousy and snippiness. I could have endured the speculation that I'd hired Daniel Crocker to kill Momma. I was regaining my senses enough to realize that Mason was the assistant DA, and there's no way on God's green earth that he'd prosecute me. I also knew Mike would never resort to bribing county officials. It might be ugly when the news broke. But we'd all clear our names in the end. All of us except Violet.

I couldn't do that to her.

I searched her worried face. Joe had always told me one day I'd have to choose—him or Violet. I just didn't know it would be this way. I took a deep breath to settle my shaky nerves. "Joe decided he wants to run for the senate, and I have to respect that. But we all know I'm not meant to be a senator's wife. It's best if we just end it now."

Violet and Neely Kate broke out into a chorus of protests, and I squeezed my eyes shut, my eyelids pushing out a fresh batch of tears. I didn't know if I could do this, but I thought of

Violet with her kids. She may have been lacking as my sister lately, but she adored her children. I could do this for her.

"Stop." My voice quivered, and I opened my eyes and forced the word out louder, "Stop."

Both women quieted.

"Look." My voice broke, and I tried again. "We all know that Joe had another life in Little Rock. He never meant to fall in love with me."

Neely Kate leaned forward, resting her hands on my knees. "No one ever plans to fall in love, Rose."

I hiccupped a breath, trying to keep from crying again. "We come from two different worlds. Who were we kidding? It was never going to work. We lived two hours away, for heaven's sake." I swallowed another sob. I had to make them believe me.

Violet frowned. "That man is head over heels in love with you. There's no way he'd just break up. He proposed."

"He changed his mind! Okay? He changed his mind." I started crying again. "He told me if we were going to stay together I had to give up my friends like Bruce Wayne and…" My voice trailed off.

"Me." Neely Kate whispered.

I shook my head, sending a jolt of pain through my already aching head. "Not just you. Everyone and everything. I'm too white trash for his family."

"*He said that?*" Violet screeched.

"No." I couldn't pin that one on him. "His mother did, though. And as much as I love Joe, he cares more about what his family wants than wanting to be with me. He still wanted to marry me, but it was clear to both of us that the person I needed to be to help him win this race isn't who I am."

"I don't believe this." Neely Kate sat back on her butt, shaking her head with narrowed eyes. "He asked you to change so he could run for the senate?"

I sighed. "We all know that I am not the ideal senator's wife."

"But he *loves* you, Rose." Violet said softly. "That man loves you with a fierceness I'd give anything to have. He wouldn't give you up unless there was a good reason."

I choked back a sob. "Sometimes love isn't enough."

"You really don't believe that do you?" Neely Kate asked.

"He left me, didn't he?" A heaved breath slipped out and I struggled to keep control of my tears. "He's gone and we just have to accept it."

"Rose—"

Violet wrapped her arm around my shoulder, but I couldn't take their pity. I stood up and looked out the window. "He was just pretending. None of this was real. Joe always told me that Joe Simmons and Joe McAllister were two different men. I just didn't realize how different." I took a breath. "This was bound to happen. We were just too stupid to admit it." My biggest fear had come true. I'd lost Joe.

I wrapped my arms around my front and held tight, thinking if I squeezed hard enough, I could keep myself from falling apart. "Joe cared about me, but he always knew it wouldn't last. That's why he kept so much of himself hidden."

Both women were silent.

I forced a laugh. "It's good this happened now. Before either of us got hurt." I started to cry again and the dam to my despair I'd spent the last several minutes building up split apart and my emotions flooded through my body. "But now I'm all alone again."

Neely Kate got up and pulled me into a hug. "You're not alone, Rose." Her voice broke with her tears. "You have me and Violet. And Mason."

Violet hugged me from behind. "You're not alone. I promise I'll make up for every awful thing I've done to you over the last few months." Her words sounded choked. "You were there for me when Mike left me. I'm here for you now."

I nodded, but we all knew it wasn't the same.

# Joe

# Chapter Two

*The night before*

I stood outside my parents' house, staring into Rose's face, dying inside after what happened at their disastrous dinner. I'd hurt her tonight. My family had done their level best to embarrass her in front of their *closest* friends, but Rose had held her head high and never let them belittle her. I'd never been so proud of anyone in my entire miserable life. Little Rose Anne Gardner from Henryetta had done what I'd always longed to do.

She'd stood up to my parents.

"What do you want to do, Joe?" She looked up at me, longing in her warm brown eyes. Whenever she looked at me like that I wanted to give her everything and anything she asked for. Because she deserved it all and so much more.

"I want to marry you." I'd just asked her to marry me moments before and I knew I'd screwed up by doing it now instead of waiting until tomorrow. It was a Hail Mary move, a panicked attempt to keep from losing her. I told myself it was okay that she didn't say yes. At least she hadn't jerked the ring off and told me to go to hell, which was exactly what I deserved. But this was Rose, who believed I was a better person, even when I knew I wasn't.

She looked back at my parents' house, and I knew what she was thinking. I lifted her chin and brought her gaze back to me. "There's only you and me. To hell with my parents. I've let them rule my life for too long. I'm going to go inside and tell them I'm done." I wanted to believe my own words, to find the strength this woman possessed. I had to believe I could stand up to them once and for all and have the life I so desperately wanted with Rose.

"What did your father say to you when he dragged you from the room?"

Reality hit me. I wasn't free to just walk in there and tell them no. My father had spent most of my lifetime building a case to use against me. And I'd done my best to provide him with the damning evidence, even if inadvertently. "He told me this was the payment for the scrapes he's gotten me out of. That I owed him."

Her eyes turned glassy. "Joe...I'm not asking you to choose."

I wanted to cry at the irony. The one person I'd gladly give up my free will to, didn't even want it. "I know. That's what makes you even more amazing. You're not the one who's insisting I choose. They are. And this time they've gone too far."

"Can you really tell him no?"

My shoulders stiffened. She voiced my own fear. "He can't force me to run for the senate."

Sadness filled her eyes and I reached for her face, desperate to prove to her that I wanted her. That I chose her. I wanted Rose more than I'd ever wanted anything in my life. "Why don't you go home, and I'll tell my parents off once and for all. I'll come home, and then tomorrow we'll start our life together."

Several emotions flickered in her eyes before she softly said, "Okay."

I kissed her, reluctant to let her leave. I wanted to get in the truck with her and drive to Henryetta, but that was the chicken-shit way out. I needed to confront my parents once and for all. "I love you, Rose. Go home, and I'll be there soon."

Rose got in the truck, but I could see the doubt in her eyes. She didn't think I was coming home to her.

I forced myself to walk into my parents' house even though everything in me screamed to run. Run after Rose. The only person who had ever seen me as the person I wanted to be, instead of the miserable excuse of a human being I really was.

Their party was in full swing when I returned to the living room. I went directly to my father and grabbed his arm. "Dad, I need to speak to you. Now."

He stopped talking to his long-time friend George White, and he turned to me, his cold eyes landing on my own. "Joe, we're talking campaign strategy. You should be part of this."

The longer I let this go on, the harder it would be to back out of it. My stomach tightened. "No, Dad. *Now.*"

His eyebrows rose, and his gaze turned deadly. I'd stared into the eyes of stone-cold killers and down the barrels of guns, but nothing had ever struck fear in me like my father's glare. Still, my back stiffened.

"J.R.," George said, patting my dad on the shoulder. "It's a big night. I'll let you have a moment with your son."

Dad's jaw locked before he swung his now smiling face back to George. "Don't be ridiculous. Joe knows whatever he has to say can wait."

"No, it can't." My voice held firm. "I'm not going to do it."

Dad's eyes widened in disbelief, and he turned his mouth toward my ear, lowering his voice so no one else could overhear. "This is neither the time nor place, Joseph. You claim you love that little tramp you trotted in her earlier tonight. If you do, you will keep your mouth shut and perform the duties expected of you. And if you don't, *you* will be the one responsible for ruining her life."

The blood rushed from my head. "What have you done?" I whispered.

His smile was as cold as his stare. "I've insured your cooperation. You know I never do anything half-ass."

My heart pounded in my ears as the men discussed campaign tactics. No, my father never did *anything* half-ass. The question was what had he done and could I undo it?

Hilary grabbed my arm and pulled me to the garden door. "You look like you need some fresh air."

Stunned, I let her lead me outside. I didn't realize where we were going until she stopped in front of the rose garden.

"Joe, I know this has all taken you by surprise tonight. Just take a moment to let it all soak in." Her voice was surprisingly soothing.

I sucked in several deep breaths.

"We've always known this day was coming. We've known it since you were ten years old. Remember? Our families were all together at dinner and your dad announced he was sending you to that summer camp for young leaders. I was upset because you were going to be gone for weeks and I couldn't bear the thought of you being gone that long. When I asked your daddy why you had to go, do you remember what he said?"

I shook my head in disgust and jerked my arm from her grasp. "What the hell are you talking about?"

"He said," her voice lowered, "'Hilary, my dear. You are looking at a future president.'"

I turned my back to her. I had no desire to relive childhood memories with the woman who did her best to screw up every good thing I'd ever had in my life. "Just shut up. I don't want to hear it."

She moved next to me and grabbed my arm. "You may not want to hear it, but it's your reality. You're almost thirty years old, Joe. It's time to grow up and accept your family responsibilities."

"This isn't what I want, Hilary, and you damn well know it."

She looked into my face with her saccharine smile. "Joe, when have our parents ever asked us what we wanted? You're lucky they let you join the state police and stay there as long as you have. Politicians are lawyers—"

I gritted my teeth. "I did my stint in law school."

She shook her head. "But you've never practiced." She spun toward the roses. "God, how many times do we have to have this conversation?"

"None!" I shouted. "I'm not having *any* conversation with you."

A scowl wrinkled her brow. "Don't be so dramatic Joe. You and I both know you're stuck with me one way or the other."

I shook my head in disbelief. "Why the hell do you even want to be with me?"

"We're meant to be together." She pivoted to watch me, moving into an alluring pose. She looked like a model and she knew it, perfectly angling her body to maximize the display of her cleavage. All it did was disgust me.

I ignored her statement about our relationship. I'd already beat that dead horse to a bloody pulp more times than I could count during the last six months. "I'm not running for the state senate. I'm telling my father off once and for all then I'm moving to Henryetta and marrying Rose."

Hilary giggled, covering her mouth and then her abdomen. "Marry Rose? Have you gone completely mental?"

My temper flared, but I kept my voice down. "This is none of your business."

"Weren't you in that dinner tonight? Did you see how awkward it was for her?"

I clenched my fists. "No thanks to you. What the hell were you doing trying to embarrass her like that?"

Hilary tilted her head with a condescending smile. "By asking her where she went to *college*? That was a *normal* question. Is your little homegrown girlfriend too fragile for a grownup conversation?"

"You and I both know that you were trying to humiliate her. She's a better person than you could ever hope to be." My body tensed with anger. "You're vile and ugly and—"

"Fine." She waved to the house. "You want to go marry that piece of white trash, march on out of this house and do it. What are you waiting for?" She shoved my chest and I stumbled backward. "Go marry her, Joe. What are you doing in the garden with me then?"

My fury burned away, fear sweeping into its place. "He has something on her."

Hilary snorted. Leave it to her to make it sound refined. "What could he possibly have on that little goody-two shoes?"

I ran a hand through my hair, nausea churning what little food I'd eaten at dinner. "I don't know." That's what scared me.

She waved her hand. "Then you have nothing to worry about."

I wasn't so sure. My father didn't make empty threats.

"You have to run in this race, Joe."

"I don't have to do anything."

"Why are you always so damn stubborn?"

"Why don't you just leave me the hell alone?"

"Because I care about you, Joe. I love you. Despite everything, I love you." She moved in front of me, her fingers wrapping around my wrists. "Do I like that you take a break from me every few months and sleep with other women? *No.*" A fire burned in her eyes. "But we're not the first couple to go through this, and we won't be the last. We can withstand anything."

I backed up out of her reach. "You and I are not together."

"Joe, you've had a rough night, and you're emotional. We'll discuss us later."

"There is no *us*, Hilary."

She moved toward me and stood on her tiptoes, kissing my cheek. "Get some rest, Joe. You have a busy month ahead of you."

I kept my gaze on the roses as the click of her heels faded.

The lights from the living room lit up the garden. The world I grew up with was in that room. The future they expected from me was in that room.

Hilary was right. What could my father have on Rose? I could walk back in the house, grab my keys, drive away, and never look back. I didn't need my parents. I didn't want them. I could walk out right now and go to the woman I loved and have the life I wanted and never see them again.

But I couldn't go.

What if he destroyed her?

My mother found me soon after, sitting on a concrete bench and staring at the roses.

"Joe, are you seriously still out here pouting?"

I cringed. "I'm waiting."

"Waiting for what?"

"For everyone to leave."

She sat down beside me. "You really have been stuck in that god-awful town too long if you can't even sit in a room and carry on a civil conversation. You need to move home as quickly as possible."

I groaned and shifted on the seat. "This is *not* my home, Mom."

Her eyes widened. "What are you talking about? Of course this is your home."

"My home is with Rose."

Mom crossed her legs, the slit of her dress exposing her shin. Her middle finger lightly tapped her thigh. "I know you think you love that girl, but she's much too simple for you, Joe."

I shook my head, my anger flaring again.

"You're young, and you've been with Hilary since the two of you were in diapers. I understand wanting something…not familiar." She shifted, her shoulders tensing. "Your father…" She cleared her throat and lifted her chin. "Let's just say I understand your *need*." She turned to me. "You're lucky that Hilary was raised in a family like ours so she's more understanding than most women. Still, there's a limit to what someone can take, Joe."

I gritted my teeth. "I don't give a *damn* about Hilary. We're over."

Her hand rested on my knee, her voice softening. "I know you blame Hilary for the unfortunate incident last spring."

My stomach twisted. "The *unfortunate incident* you refer to has a name, mother. Her name was Savannah."

Her fingers gently patted my leg. "Yes, of course dear. I know."

I felt like I was going to be sick. "She deserves more respect than that."

"Joe, dredging up those dreadful memories doesn't do anyone any good. What's done is done. We can only move on."

"Savannah can't move on."

"No, she can't, but that doesn't mean that you shouldn't." She sighed and leaned closer. "I understand Rose's appeal. I really do. She's a simple girl, and she asks little of you, am I right? You can be with her and act like you're on an undercover assignment, pretending to be someone else. But you're fooling yourself, Joe. You are *not* some redneck good ol' boy who can live in rural Arkansas as a sheriff's deputy." She shook her head. "A sheriff's deputy in Fenton County? *Really*, Joe?"

She tsked, and I felt the uncertainty that had plagued me my entire life, making me question every choice I'd ever made that wasn't sanctioned by my parents. "She's a good person, Mom. She loves me for me."

"Of course she does, Joe. I bet she'd be happy with you being a deputy and getting married and raising a house full of kids. But you were destined for bigger things. She's easy for you to be with because she expects so little of you. You needed that after your recent... trauma. You needed someone to let you heal, and I admit, what little I know of the girl and your relationship, she's been a wonderful distraction."

"She is not a distraction."

"Joseph, we need someone who challenges us to become a better person."

My voice broke. "She *does* make me want to be a better person."

"That's not what I meant and you know it. You were born to inherit great power and it comes with a price. With great responsibility comes great sacrifice."

"I never asked for any of this."

"No, you didn't, but you were born into it anyway. Did King Louis XVI ask to be born into a family that predestined him to be king?"

"Are you *seriously* comparing me to a king of France?"

She grabbed my arm. "Joseph, you have your place in this world and Henryetta, Arkansas isn't it."

She was good. As always, she twisted my words and made me question everything. But there was one thing my mother couldn't make me doubt. "I love her."

"I'm sure that you think you do."

I turned to her, my emotion flowing to the surface. "I *love* her. I've never loved *anyone* like I love her."

She studied me then a soft smile covered her face, reminding me of the woman who loved me when I was a small boy. Before she jumped onto my father's train to be make me the next great American politician. "Yes, I think you really do." She turned back to the house. "I need to say goodbye to our remaining guests then we'll discuss this with your father."

Relief washed through me, and I nodded. I might have swayed her to my side.

"But you need to come in and make an appearance. Your father announced your candidacy, and you're hiding in the garden like a sulking child."

She was right, but I wasn't sure what else to do. I couldn't stay in there and pretend to accept his announcement, and to publically embarrass him could ultimately hurt Rose. I stood and my shoulders tensed. "I just want to get this over with."

Looping her arm around mine, Mom pulled me toward the house and murmured, "Be careful what you wish for."

# Chapter Three

I followed my mother into their soirée, thanking the guests for attending then claiming I needed to get busy with the campaign. My father shot me a look of disapproval as I left to wait in the study, but I didn't care. I wasn't going through with this masquerade. All I wanted was for him to come in and tell me what he had on Rose so I could go home and figure out how to protect her.

Funny how I always thought of Rose's house as home now, but why wouldn't I? My mother claimed this was my home, but it had never been home. Once I turned eight, I'd been raised by housekeepers and tutors. This house was like a museum with all its antiques and stiff formality. My mother would turn up her nose if she walked into Rose's tiny house, but when I looked back on the last twenty-nine years, I knew it didn't matter what was in the house. It was the love that filled it. The only real home I'd ever known was when I was with Rose.

I went into my father's study to wait, reliving my moments with Rose in the room hours earlier. God, I'd hurt her so badly. My shame burned a hole in my chest. How could she still want me? Yet she did. Her love was unconditional.

I'd told her about Savannah, but there was so much more I wasn't proud of. So much more that I hoped Rose would never know about, so she wouldn't look at me the way she had after I told her my secret. With horror and disbelief.

I'd never known anyone like Rose, let alone hoped to have someone like her love me. Hell, I'd never thought someone could ever love me without wanting something in return. My parents expected me to continue the family legacy. Hilary thought I'd be a rising political star and wanted to be on my arm. Even my sister expected me to break free from my parents' hold and refused to talk to me when I didn't do it her way.

Everyone wanted something from me. Everyone except for Rose. She loved me for me, or the me I showed her. The only thing she expected in return was for me to love her back. I spent the first two months of our relationship waiting for her to realize that I was nothing but a fraud and break up with me. But she didn't. She only saw the good and never assumed I was anything less, even when I tried to tell her Joe Simmons wasn't the man she knew. She thought I was deluded for even suggesting such a thing. And I let myself believe her. I let myself believe that I really was the man she knew, that when I left Little Rock, I became Joe McAllister, a simple man who wanted nothing but the woman he loved and a family. The rest of the world be damned.

But it was all a lie, and the deeper I got into a relationship with her, the more anxious I became that the house of cards would come tumbling down, and I'd lose her.

It didn't help that I knew Mason Deveraux was waiting in the wings, ready to clean up the mess I'd eventually leave. He'd told me once in Little Rock that he was a patient man. He may have been referring to Savannah, but I knew it filled every part of his life. And Rose was definitely worth waiting for.

But I still clung to the hope it would all work out. That I could spend the rest of my life with Rose Gardner through better or worse, till death do us part. I had to believe it because when I thought of the alternative, panic clawed at my insides, ripping my hope to shreds. I couldn't accidently stumble upon Rose in god-forsaken Henryetta, Arkansas, just to lose her.

Mom was right. Rose didn't expect more from me like they did. The only thing she wanted from me was to be happy. Why did Mom make it sound so colloquial?

The study door opened and my mother came in with my father following behind her. He filled the threshold, pausing for effect. It was a move I was long familiar with and even though I recognized it for what it was, the same uneasy fear from my childhood crept through my body, a metallic taste coating my tongue. Some reactions were long since conditioned into me. The switch he used to hold in his hand had helped reenforce it.

"You embarrassed me tonight, Joseph."

My back stiffened and I stuffed down my dread. It was time I finally took control and stood up to him. I was nearly thirty years old. "I embarrassed you? What do you think you and Mom did to Rose?"

His eyes clouded with confusion. "Rose? What the hell does she have to do with anything?"

"She's the woman I love. The woman I want to spend the rest of my life with. The way you treat her is *everything* to me."

My father's face reddened. "I did not spend twenty-nine years grooming you for this to let you throw it away for a backwoods girl from Fenton County."

I took a step toward him, my anger flushing my skin. "If you think I'm going to stand here and listen to you insult her, you've got another thing coming."

"Joe." Mom grabbed my arm and drawled. "You have to acknowledge our concern. How do you know this girl doesn't want you for your money?"

"Because she didn't even know I had money until July!"

My father growled, "It doesn't matter whether she wants your money or not, she's not acceptable."

"I don't give a shit if you find her acceptable or not. I've asked her to marry me and there's not a damn thing you can do about it."

His body tensed. "You won't be marrying her if she's in prison."

My blood fled to my feet. "What the hell are you talking about?"

"Have a seat, Joe." My father brushed past me and moved behind his desk.

I spun around to face him. "I don't want to have a seat. What I have to say can be said just fine standing."

Dad sat in his chair and glared at me. "Have a *seat*, Joseph."

I lowered to the seat in front of his desk while my mother sank into the chair next to me.

"If you think you have something to put her in jail, you're either deluded or you've fabricated evidence." I swallowed the bile rising in my throat. "I'm going with the latter."

My father leaned back in his seat. "Monroe Peterman called about ten minutes ago with something that could be an issue."

"I don't give a damn what Monroe Peterman had to say. I want to know what you have on Rose."

He shook his head in disgust. "You *should* be worried about what Monroe Peterman had to say instead of that girl. You have a challenger in the senate race."

I paused. Maybe I could still get out of this. "You said I would be unopposed."

"And you were supposed to be, but I just got word that Delany's going to announce his candidacy tomorrow morning."

"So I don't need to run now."

Dad banged his fist on the desk. "Of course you're going to run! But it means we have to put a hell of a lot more effort into this than we originally planned."

"Delany's a big family man," Mom mumbled, her nails clicking on the arm of her chair. "He plays that to the hilt. He'll take advantage of his kids in soccer and Boy Scouts. It could be an issue that Joe's not married."

"I'm not running!" I shouted.

My father's face reddened. "Like hell you won't. This is what we've been preparing you to do since the doctor slapped your behind in the delivery room. This is the perfect opportunity to jump in. So what if Delany's a family man? He's bound to turn off some of the voters with his ultraconservative Christian fundamentalism."

"I'm not so sure, J.R.," Mom said. "Joe's being single could be a bigger issue than you think."

I fought to maintain what little control I had left. "I'm not running."

My father turned his gaze on me. "Do you really want to see that little piece of fluff in jail? I'm not so sure how long she'd last in there."

"You keep saying that, but so far, you've produced nothing. You're bluffing." I wanted to tell him that she was stronger than he gave her credit for, but I couldn't see how that would help my case.

Dad opened a desk drawer and pulled out a small stack of papers, slapping them on the desk and sliding them toward me.

"Bluffing, huh? You check those out and tell me if we should continue this discussion."

I picked up the stack, a cold sweat beading on the back of my neck. He had papers that suggested Violet's husband Mike had bribed county officials to support his construction company. Next he had photos of Violet sneaking out of a hotel with the new mayor of Henryetta. I studied the photos, wondering how he'd gotten those staged. If they were Photoshopped, whoever had done it did a damn good job. But the last sent ice through my veins. I held a bank account statement in Rose's name with a wire transfer into an account with Daniel Crocker's name. Fifty thousand dollars dated a week before her mother's murder.

I looked up at him, trying to contain my fear. "This will never hold up. You and I both know that."

"Are you willing to bet her life on it? From what I hear, she doesn't have that great of reputation in that town. I suspect they'll believe this hook, line, and sinker. They had no qualms believing she killed her mother during their initial investigation."

My hand shook, giving away my fear. "Not Mason. He'll never buy it."

"Mason Deveraux?" My father laughed. "I put him in that hell hole, and I can pull him out of it. And all behind the scenes, so that he never even knows. The DA and that Judge McClary will do what I want."

I shoved the papers onto his desk. "Don't take Mason Deveraux for a fool. He'll never stand back and let you do this."

"No one lets me do anything, least of all a lowly assistant DA who has a job because I deemed fit to make sure he had one. Don't delude yourself into thinking you can stop me, Joe. Are you really willing to risk it?"

I gripped the edge of the chair, my knuckles turning white. "What the hell do you want? That I run in this asinine race?" I swallowed, trying to settle my frayed nerves. "Fine. I'll run, but I'm still marrying Rose."

His lips pursed with a scowl. "Not acceptable."

"The only way I do this is with her. I know you find this impossible to believe, but I actually love her. Genuine love, not the political for-show marriage you and Mom put on."

"Joseph," Mom gasped.

"Genuine love?" Dad shouted. "What the hell does love have to do with *anything*? You marry for money and power. Hell, even that Fenton County tart has figured that one out." He took a breath to settle down. "I've tolerated your rebellion for years thinking, 'let the boy get it out of his system before he runs for office.' We couldn't have you creating a scandal once your political career began, so we gave you a free rein. Overachiever that you are, you've done your level best to sow as many wild oats as there are fields to plant 'em in. You, me, and God only know the messes you've created that I've cleaned up over the years. But I did it, literally banking on the payoff at the end." He pointed his finger at me, the veins on his temple throbbing. "*You owe me, Joe.* I've been cleaning up your shit for years, and now it's time to pony up, boy. And I swear to God and all that is holy, if you don't, *I will bury that girl.*"

I stood, my stomach rolling, and I took in several deep breaths as fear flooded every cell of my body. I wanted to protest that she was innocent, and that she'd never done anything to him, but when had that ever stopped him before? J.R. Simmons was ruthless.

My mother watched me, a war of emotion battling on her face.

I swallowed a cry of anguish. What the hell had I expected? He was right. I'd created more scandals than a person had a right to. I might have sailed out of every single one unscathed, yet with every transgression, I was one foot deeper in my father's pit. I'd dug the very hole I was trapped in.

I walked over to my father's minibar and poured a glass of whiskey, taking a gulp.

"J.R.," Mom said softly. "I'm telling you, he'll never win against Delany."

"What the Sam Hill are you talking about, Betsy?" My father bellowed.

"You're not giving the family angle enough credit. Not in this district. Not where sponsoring your local Little League team can increase your business fivefold."

I took another swig, letting the liquid warm its way down my throat.

"And what the hell do you want to do about that?" he asked.

My mother hesitated. "Let him make his engagement public."

I swung around to face her.

My father's stunned face gaped at both of us. "To that....that..."

I slammed the glass down on the table. "*Her name is Rose,*" I forced out through gritted teeth. I took a step toward him. "And she is good and decent and a better person than you could ever hope to be."

He shook his head with a sneer. "That may be true, but we all know what they say about nice guys finishing last and the same applies to her." He rested his forearms on his desk and leaned forward. "She may be good and decent, but you need cunning and resourceful. You need Hilary."

I shook my head, barely containing my horror. I'd always known this day of reckoning was coming, but I'd never had anything worth standing up for against him. Not before Rose. But then again, that was exactly why he chose now to spring this on me. When I had too much to lose to say no. "I will *never* marry Hilary." My voice shook with emotion.

"J.R.," my mother pleaded. "Listen to me. You can use that Fenton County girl to your advantage. She's lower class like half the population of the county he'll represent. Delany's going to use his humble roots against our money as well as play the family angle." She scooted forward in her seat, resting her hand on the desk. "Let Joe try a test engagement with her. He can use her small business as an example to support your small business program. He can trot her out on the campaign trail with him, and she can swap coon recipes with people like her." Her eyes burned bright. "We can *use* this, J.R."

My father's eyes narrowed on me. "Did you put her up to this?"

My mouth dropped. "You're asking me this after she did everything in her power to embarrass Rose at dinner?"

Mom's face hardened. "If I had used everything in my power, that girl would have crawled out of here on her hands and knees. Don't take my suggestion as a confirmation nor acceptance of this girl as a suitable wife for you. But if life hands you lemons, you squeeze the hell out of them to get what you want. Why should this be any different?" Her gaze turned to Dad. "In this case, she might help Joe garner more votes. The lower socioeconomic-class voters will feel an affinity with her, much more so than Frank Delany's wife. And we both know that the spouse—or in this case, potential spouse—is just as important as the candidate."

My father paused as he considered her words. "You might be right."

My pulse pounded in my head.

Encouraged, Mom continued. "She will need to be schooled. We'll teach her proper manners and improve her look without making her too made-up."

I glared. "There is absolutely nothing wrong with how she looks!"

She rolled her eyes. "Stop thinking with the appendage in your pants for *once* in your life, Joseph. We're giving you want you want, even if on a trial basis, so show a little appreciation. We'll see how she does and how the voters react. But I'm warning you, if she doesn't help your campaign, she's history."

I took several shallow breaths.

"She'll have to stop associating with half that town though. Most are derelicts and imbeciles. She's hired the town drug addict, for heaven sakes. She'll need to fire him at once, lest she tarnish what little she has left of her reputation." A tiny smile curled up her lips. "That will be a condition of acceptance for us. If she can't follow this rule, then she is done before she even starts."

Conditions. Of course. When had I ever been given any gift from my parents that didn't come with conditions.

"She can continue to work at her nursery, but on a more limited basis. She'll be expected to campaign with you at least half the time."

"Anything else?" I asked in a sarcastic tone.

"She will be expected to meet our standards of behavior and dress. If she does not comply, she will be removed."

"Be removed? You make her sound like a vase of dying flowers."

Her brow lifted with a sardonic stare. "An appropriate analogy if I ever heard one."

"You expect me to discard the woman I love if she doesn't live up to your political expectations?"

Her eyes turned cold. "Yes."

"If she doesn't work out, keep her as mistress," Dad volunteered.

"A mistress? I would never belittle her by keeping her as a *mistress*." I spat in disgust. "She deserves a hell of a lot more than that."

"Then you better hope she works out."

"Am I done?" I asked sarcastically.

Dad snorted. "You are far from done. You've only just begun."

Mom waved her hand dismissively. "Go. I know you want to go to her tonight and you need to get this ironed out before we make your official announcement tomorrow."

My father pushed his chair back. "But I expect you back by eleven tomorrow morning. And tell your girlfriend that she is indefinitely on call until this campaign is in the bag."

# Chapter Four

The closer I got to Henryetta, the more nervous I became. What I had originally seen as a victory I quickly realized was a thorn-covered crown. There was no way Rose would agree to any of it.

I was going to lose her anyway.

I stuffed down my fear. I would tell her the truth and let her decide. I couldn't make her agree to anything, but I knew she loved me and would do anything for me. Even in my desperation, I knew it wasn't fair to ask, but I'd finally found the one person I couldn't live without. I wasn't ready to give her up without trying.

When I pulled onto Rose's street, the police car in front of her house sent a new fear coursing through my blood. I parked in front of Mildred's house and ran across the street as Ernie walked out Rose's front door.

"Where is she?" I choked out.

He shot me a surprised look. "The hospital."

I stopped in my tracks, panic flooding my head. "*What happened?*"

"She was kidnapped. She'd called 9-1-1 but by the time we arrived here, she was already gone. The assistant DA called and told us she was at Reverend Pruitt's house."

"Is she okay?"

"I didn't see her, but she didn't go in an ambulance so that has to be a good sign. Deveraux took her."

*Mason*. My anger simmered. What the hell was he up to? But I knew. It didn't take a genius to figure it out.

"What about her dog?"

"That little thing that looks like an overgrown rat? It was shut up in the bathroom, barking loud enough to wake the neighbors."

I breathed a sigh of relief. I loved that dog as much as Rose did. "Thanks. Make sure she's okay, and I'll be back later."

I got in my car and made a quick call to Detective Taylor who filled me in on the basic facts during my short drive to the hospital. Jonah Pruitt's secretary was actually his mother and had confessed to murdering the elderly women. She'd also kidnapped Rose with the intention of killing her. But Mason had figured out where Rose was and had reached her in time.

How in the hell did Rose get mixed up in that?

But that was Rose. She'd been in more scrapes in the four months since I met her than any other person I knew. How in the world could I make her part of my campaign? Especially with her visions?

Fear washed through me making me numb. I was going to lose her.

Anger quickly swooped in to replace my fear. Anger at Rose for putting herself in danger. Anger at Mason for being there for her when I couldn't. Anger at my parents for their ultimatums and expectations. But most of all, anger at myself. I had no one to blame for the position I was in but me. If I hadn't lived the life I had, my parents wouldn't have leverage to hold over my head.

My anger raged to a boiling point by the time I got to the hospital. When I approached the emergency room desk, I snarled, "Rose Gardner. Where is she?"

The receptionist looked up startled. "I'm sorry. We can't share that information."

I pulled out my wallet and flashed my state police badge. "Happy? *Now where the hell is she?*"

Flustered, she stood. "She's in the back." She opened the locked door and stood to the side as I barged through.

"Where is she?"

"Exam room four." Her voice shook. "But she might still be in X-ray."

I stormed down the hall, stopping outside room four when I heard voices.

"Everything go okay?" Mason's voice was clear as an aide opened the door, giving me an odd look as he left the room.

"It was fine." Rose answered, sounding tired. "They said they'd tell me the results soon."

Mason was still with her. But why wouldn't he be? When we'd worked together in July to get her out of lockup, it had been obvious that he had an interest in her that wasn't platonic. Amazingly enough, after I'd asked him to stay away from her, he'd complied until Rose put two-and-two together. And after she knew about our arrangement, he probably figured all bets were off. But now that I'd gotten the deputy sheriff position, I'd be the one with her. I'd be the one she could rely on.

Only I wouldn't be. I'd be running for the state senate and Fenton County was outside the district I was running in.

My anger resurfaced.

I had my hand on the wooden door, ready to barge in when I heard Rose say, "Mason, you don't have to stay with me. Go home and go to bed."

"Someone has to make sure you get home okay," Mason's voice was warm and reassuring.

And that was the icing on the cake. The last reminder that he'd be the one to watch out for her when I was gone. I shoved the door open. I might lose her, but I hadn't lost her yet. "Yeah, that someone is me."

Rose looked up startled, while Mason turned a cold stare on me. I could handle Mason Deveraux. He was *nothing* compared to my father.

But when I got a good look at Rose's face, I stopped in my tracks. She was bruised and dried blood covered the side of her face, neck, and chest, and the slip she was wearing. I forced myself to take a breath. "What happened?"

She offered me a tight smile. "Oh, you know. The usual. Kidnapping, attempted murder."

She could have been killed and I should have been with her but instead, I was listening to my parents and their damn expectations. "Are you okay?"

"I'm fine. Really. Just bruised and banged up."

This was never going to work. Finding her like this was proof enough. All it would take would be one incident like this to cause a scandal and my parents would toss her out onto the street, probably making sure to ruin her before she even landed just to ensure she'd never be back. Grief and panic bolstered my anger. "How did this happen. Again? Why can't you leave these things alone?"

Rose looked shell-shocked, making me feel like an even bigger ass.

Mason stood, turning at a defensive angle. "I don't like how you're talking to her."

Mason Deveraux was protecting Rose from me? It was all I could do not to beat the shit out of him. "What are you still doing here? When did it become the job of the prosecuting attorney to hold a vigil with a victim?"

"Joe," Rose said, her voice tight.

She was almost killed tonight and she was trying to downplay it. And Mason Deveraux was standing there encouraging her. "She doesn't think about the consequences of what she's doing, and you damn well know I'm right."

Mason tensed, moving closer to her. "Are you suggesting that she brings this on herself?"

He was still trying to protect her. *From me.* I forced myself to calm down. "I'm saying she's going to get herself killed if she doesn't stop and think about her own safety."

Mason took several breaths and looked like he was about to punch me. "Perhaps if you were actually here to witness what goes on in her life, you'd see that she did nothing to bring any of this upon herself."

He wasn't saying anything I didn't already know, but it still didn't set well. Especially when Mason was the one who had replaced me. "You've made damn sure you're close at hand, haven't you, Deveraux?"

Mason's eyes narrowed, his own rage riding close to the surface. He moved next the bed. "I'm not doing this to Rose tonight. She's been through too much trauma." He kissed Rose's forehead, and it was all I could do to not tear him away from her and toss him out the door. "You know how to find me if you need me."

"Thanks, Mason." She smiled at him with gratitude.

Of course she looked at him with gratitude. From what Taylor told me, Deveraux had literally saved her life. What was going to happen to her when I wasn't with her? When I had to walk away from her. Because I knew that was the decision I ultimately had to face, even if I wasn't ready to do it yet. The fact remained that if Mason hadn't saved her, I wouldn't be standing here needing to make that decision. I'd be going to her funeral.

I turned away, unable to face the love of my life and the man who would almost certainly replace me. "Thank you." It was all I could do to keep from breaking down. I cleared the lump from my throat. "Thank you for saving her."

Mason moved to the doorway and stopped in the threshold. "I'll always be there for Rose when she needs me."

His words only drove the knife deeper.

When he left, I sat next to her, wondering how physically hurt she really was. I couldn't imagine losing her, yet I couldn't find a way to avert this disaster. I picked up her hand, the ring on her finger filling me with sadness. "You're still wearing my ring."

"Yeah."

I blinked to keep from crying. "What happened tonight?" She didn't answer me and I stroked the back of her hand. "Detective Taylor said Jonah's mother kidnapped you and threatened to kill you."

She shifted, uncomfortable talking about it. "That sounds about right."

"I told you that Jonah Pruitt was trouble."

"Jonah Pruitt is the furthest thing from trouble I've met in ages. He's just as much a victim as those poor women are."

One more piece of evidence that proved I had to let her go. There was no way she could turn her back on someone who needed help, and I was a bastard to even consider asking her. "You collect them don't you? You can't help yourself."

She looked up in surprise. "What are you talking about?"

"The outcasts. Bruce Wayne. Jonah Pruitt…"

She sat up, a fire in her eyes. "If you add Neely Kate to that list, I'm liable to hurt you." Her gaze leveled on me. "When did you get back to Henryetta?"

"Just a few minutes ago."

She glanced at the clock. "But it's almost two in the morning. Have you been with your parents this entire time?"

"Yes." I knew I had to tell her what happened but I couldn't bring myself to do it yet. Not here. Not now. But it was inevitable. I had to be back in El Dorado by eleven tomorrow.

"You're running for the senate aren't you?" Her voice was so quiet I could barely hear her.

I remained silent, not trusting myself to speak.

"What about us?"

I couldn't do it. I couldn't lose her. I'd fight this. I'd find a way to salvage this mess. I picked up her hand and gently kissed her palm, my will to fight blazing a path through my body. "What about us? I still want to marry you, Rose. Nothing's changed there."

"I'd make a terrible politician's wife, Joe. What if I have a vision at an important event? What if people ask me about my education?"

"Not everyone is like my parents."

She started to cry, and I wanted to kill my father, strangle him with my bare hands. He'd done this to her. To us. But that didn't help Rose. I wiped the tears from her cheeks, careful around her bruises. "Don't cry, Rose. Nothing's going to change the way I feel about you. I don't care what anyone says." But I knew it didn't matter how I felt. My parents didn't care.

Rose looked up at me, fear in her eyes. "I want to have a vision."

My mouth dropped open. "Of me?"

She nodded.

"But you hate doing that."

"I tried one on purpose today, and now I want to try it with you."

I picked up her hand. "Okay." This was good. Why hadn't I thought of it myself? She could see my future and see us together, giving me the reassurance I needed to find a way to save us.

Her eyes sank closed, and her body stilled while I clung to her for dear life. But when her eyes flew open, she started to cry again, her words gargled with her tears.

Terror shot through my body. "What did you see?"

She tried to catch her breath. "You won."

"The senate race?" I didn't care about that. I wanted to know about us.

"I don't know about this one. The one I saw was for the U.S. Senate."

What had she really seen? "Are you really that upset about me running for office?"

"No, there's more."

If she was this distraught, I didn't want to know. But I'd spent my life making messes and letting my father clean them up. I needed to face this head-on. Then maybe I could change it. "Okay."

"You were married. To someone else." Her tear-filled eyes searched mine, and her voice broke. "You were married to Hilary, and she was pregnant."

Shock and horror flooded my head and I stood. "*No!*"

She watched me in silence.

This was a nightmare come true. "I love *you*, Rose." I could hardly talk past the lump in my throat. She was blurry through my tears. "I don't love her."

Rose watched me, tears streaming down her face.

She believed it would come true.

The embers of my anger were stoked into another roaring fire. "You know damn good and well that what you see doesn't always come true. What was the vision you saw earlier?"

"My murder tonight. Rhonda shot me in the head."

"Oh, God." She'd seen her own murder? Panic replaced my anger, and I took her in my arms, terrified. "Why didn't you tell me?"

"There wasn't time with the dinner and the announcement. Besides, I couldn't see my face, so I didn't know it was me until Mason called to check on me, and I told him there was someone outside and the police weren't coming." She paused, her voice cracking. "I think we both knew it was similar to what happened to his sister."

Mason had called her tonight. How close had they gotten over the last few days? "So you talked about his side of things."

"We're friends, Joe. If it weren't for Mason, I really would be dead right now."

The door opened behind me and a doctor walked into the room. Her gaze swung around, looking surprised when it landed on me. "Ms. Gardner, we have good news. There's no sign of concussion, but we'll need to stitch up your head wound. It's close to your hairline, so the scar should be hidden."

She examined Rose's back to reveal large bruises and I forced myself not to gasp at the purple welts. Jonah Pruitt's mother had hurt her, and I hadn't been there to protect her.

The doctor left the room saying someone would be back to stitch Rose's head.

Rose looked into my face, a sad acceptance in her eyes. "You're right. My vision didn't entirely come true. But a lot of it did."

I wanted to scream. If Rose didn't believe in us, we were lost. "We can change it, Rose."

"Do you care about her?"

"We've known each other for a long time, so it's hard not to hope she's okay. But we're over. Your vision is wrong."

"Do you want to run for the senate, Joe? If your father and I weren't involved, what would you want to do?"

I sat down. I should tell her everything. Seek her advice. But Rose didn't back down from trouble, her battered body was proof enough of that. I wasn't sure I could put her through it. I took the chicken-shit way out. "I think I can make a difference."

Rose looked like she wanted to say something but someone came in to put in her stitches.

We were silent most of the way home. Rose was exhausted, and I was too heartbroken to speak.

I helped her inside and off with her bloody dress and into one of my T-shirts. I tucked her into bed and then took Muffy outside.

The little dog was excited to see me and I sat down on the front steps, rubbing the back of her head. "I'm going to miss you, Muff." Muffy may have been Rose's dog, but I always felt like she was part mine too. I buried my face in her fur. "It had to be a rough night for you." I checked her over to make sure she hadn't gotten hurt when Rose was attacked. I knew how protective she was of Rose. But she seemed just fine and I sent her into the yard, surprised I'd miss this along with everything else I associated with Rose.

After Muffy did her business, I took her inside and stripped down to my boxers and slipped into bed next to Rose. She was on her side, turned away from me so she wasn't lying on her stitches. I carefully pressed my stomach to her back, wrapping my arms around her waist.

"I love you, Rose." I kissed her neck.

Her voice broke. "I love you too."

I couldn't believe this was my last night with her. I took a breath to keep from crying. Tomorrow I had to break both of our hearts all over again.

# Chapter Five

Sunlight woke me up and I snuggled into Rose, dozing before reality hit me.

Today was the day I had to let her go.

I lay in bed, studying the curve of her mouth, the contrast of her dark eyelashes against her creamy skin. I picked up several strands of her dark hair. Soon after her mother had been killed, her aunt had cut her hair to a little past her shoulders, but it had grown out since.

I watched her, wishing she was naked so I could take one last memory of that part of her too. The weight of her breasts in my hand, her legs wrapped around me when we made love. I closed my eyes, pushing down my grief. I had a lifetime to live with the pain. For now, I just wanted to embrace this time with her.

But Muffy was dancing around the room, begging to go out. I eased myself out of bed, careful to not disturb Rose. I threw on a spare pair of clothes I kept there, realizing I had to pack up my things.

I wasn't sure I could leave her, but I didn't have a choice.

I checked my phone and Rose's while I took Muffy out. Violet had called Rose almost a dozen times since last night. She'd probably heard about the kidnapping and needed to make sure Rose was okay. I called her from my phone, and she jumped all over me the moment she realized who she was talking to.

"Why didn't someone tell me that Rose was in trouble last night?"

"I don't know, Violet. I didn't get to the hospital until almost two a.m. and by the time she got checked out, it was too late to call." I took Muffy back inside and surveyed the cabinets for food. Who would shop for Rose when I was gone? She never thought to get anything for herself. She'd live off of turkey sandwiches and cereal.

"What happened?" Violet demanded.

"I don't know all the details, Violet. I told you, I didn't get here until she was in the hospital."

Rose appeared in the doorway, my T-shirt hitting her thighs and her sexy legs peeking out. Her hair draped over her shoulders and partly covered the bruises on her face. The sight of her sent blood rushing to my groin.

"You didn't save her from that crazy woman?" Violet asked.

I tried to stuff down the bitterness that I owed Rose's life to Mason and tried to focus on my thankfulness. I really did owe him, as hard as it was to swallow. "No. Mason knew where to find her. He got to her before the police."

Rose moved toward me, her bare feet padding across the floor. I reached for her, pulling her to my chest and kissing her head, breathing in the scent of her. God, I loved her smell, a mixture of her shampoo and the flowers she worked with.

She looked up at me and mouthed. "Thank you."

I could mope for the rest of the time I had left, or I could make the best of it. For both of us. I forced a grin and mouthed, "You can repay me later."

A soft smile of happiness spread across her face.

"Well, is she okay?" Violet asked.

"She won't be in for the rest of the day. She still has to give a *lengthy* police statement." I gave her a playful look. "Apparently, she's about to supply them with all the evidence Deveraux needs to try this case." That God damned Henryetta police department had to be the biggest band of fools ever assembled. I wanted to blame them for this mess too. "But even when she's done, she needs to rest. She's pretty beat up."

I finally got Violet off the phone and turned it to vibrate before I tossed it on the table. I sure as hell didn't want my father calling me before I was ready to leave. It was a little after nine so that meant I still had an hour with her.

I lifted Rose's chin, tilting her face from side to side. "You look more beat up on the right side, but it obviously could have been much worse. And you have two horrible bruises on your back. You need to take it easy today."

"If it means I get to spend the day with you, it sounds wonderful."

All the happiness I had mustered fled. "I'm going to have to run back to El Dorado in about an hour."

Sadness crept into her eyes. "So you're really doing this?"

"Yeah," I whispered. Should I tell her now? Was I just dragging this out for both of us?

She wrapped my arms around my neck and snuggled into my chest, sadness oozing from her pores. "What about the sheriff's deputy job?"

*Tell her. She deserves the truth.* But she was in my arms and I wanted every moment I had left with her. If that made me a selfish bastard, so be it. "That's on hold for now."

Rose pulled away and turned to the counter. "I need coffee."

My heart burst with grief. "I'm going to make you breakfast too."

"If you're leaving in an hour, I'd rather just spend the time with you."

"Okay," I said softly.

There was a rap on the front door and she jumped. She had every right to be jumpy after last night. I trailed my fingers up and down her arm. "I'll get it."

When I opened the door, I recognized Bruce Wayne Decker. He looked like the man who'd been on trial, yet he was different somehow.

He looked at me and swallowed, but held his head high. "Is Rose here?"

"Yeah."

"Can I speak to her?"

There was a confidence in him that hadn't been there before. I had no doubt that Rose had done that for him. She'd given him a job and believed in him when no one else had. Pride blossomed in my chest, and I cleared my throat to speak. "I'll get her."

She was pouring a bowl of cereal when I walked in. "Rose, it's for you."

"Oh." She looked worried when she walked to the front door.

I grimaced at the cereal then pulled out the last of the eggs to make her a quick omelet.

I had to tell her the truth. She deserved to know, yet I was also smart enough to know she was like a pole cat. She'd stand up to my father to the bitter end. But I owed her the choice. I couldn't make it for her. A small part of me hoped she'd agree to all the terms, but the rest of me was horrified at the thought. Even if it meant losing her.

"I told you that you didn't have to cook, Joe," she said when she came back several minutes later.

I twisted to see her sit at the table. "I know darlin', but I wanted to make sure you ate something filling, something that's not cereal." I pulled a plate out of the cabinet and slid the omelet onto it, and set it on the table.

She took a bite and kept her gaze on her plate. "Go ahead and spill it. I can always tell when you're worried."

I'd hoped to put this off and spend more time with her. I'd hoped to make love to her one more time, but I knew the kindest thing I could do was to get this over with now. I'd tell her the truth. Maybe I'd tell her the terms, and she'd throw me out before I got to the part about my father threatening her and her family. If I looked like a bastard, so be it. Maybe it would make it easier for her. "This senate race might be tight."

She still didn't look up. "I thought the race was unopposed."

"Someone else is going to declare he's running later this morning. Frank Delany. Delany's a family man, so they'll be comparing me to him."

She hesitated. "Is that why you asked me to marry you?"

"No. God, no." I picked up her hand and searched her face. "I told you that I planned to ask you today. Before I knew about the senate race."

"What does that have to do with what you're worried about?"

"My mother is concerned."

She put her fork down.

"You're from a lower socioeconomic class than the opponent."

She tensed. "And you." She finally raised her gaze. "I'm *much* lower than you."

"But we can spin that as a positive. Look at the nursery that you and Violet started. Voters love that kind of stuff. I told my mother that you might actually be an advantage. We can pull in voters who relate to you and your humble roots."

She sat up straighter. "I believe your mother called it 'poor white trash.'"

I flinched. Had mom insulted her before dinner when I was with Hilary or after when Dad dragged me from the dining room? Did it matter?

"Why are you doing this?"

I stared into her face. I should just let her go, but selfish bastard that I was, I couldn't do it.

"Where's my Joe?" Tears filled her voice. "Because he would never talk about using me for votes."

I closed my eyes and shook my head. "That all came out wrong. I'm doing this all wrong."

"Joe McAllister couldn't give two figs about a political office. Joe McAllister wanted to be with me and barbeque and take picnics and walk Muffy."

Desperation billowed in my chest as I looked out the window. Not only would she not agree to this, she was going to hate me. I told myself that was for the best but the thought of her hating me sent a jolt of pain through my chest.

"Your mother called me a pretty diversion from all the bad things that had happened to you this year." She paused. "Is that true? Is that what I am to you?"

"God, no." My eyes burned. "How can you ask that?" I squeezed her hand in my despair. "Do you even know how much I love you?"

"You know, you were right." She sat back in her chair. "You're very obviously two different men. Joe McAllister—my Joe—and Joe Simmons—the man you've fought so hard not to be. You're turning back into him."

Her words stung, and I couldn't hide my bitterness. "You're the one who told me there was only one me."

She took a deep breath. "So you plan on using the story of our entrepreneurial spirit in the campaign?"

"If you agree."

"What else do you want me to do?"

Was she really open to this? "You'll need to distance yourself from characters like Bruce Wayne and David for a while."

"And what about Neely Kate?"

I snuck a glance at her. She sounded surprising emotionless at the suggestion. "I'm not sure yet."

"So I need to cut the few friends I have out of my life. Mason too?"

I couldn't answer her. I was asking her to give up everything. For *me*. I sure as hell didn't deserve it, and she didn't deserve the misery it would put her through.

"I guess I can work at the nursery since it will help your campaign."

Was she really considering it? "For a while anyway, until we get married. We can't live in Henryetta since it's not in the same jurisdiction." I squeezed her hand so hard I had to have cut off her circulation. "I guess we'll live in El Dorado when we're not in Little Rock."

"Okay."

I stared at her in disbelief. She was going to do it. While part of me was ecstatic, the rest of me was horrified. "Okay?" I dropped her hand and stood in front of the sink, grabbing hold of the counter. "Are you *even listening* to what I'm asking you to do?" I spun around to face her. "Are you seriously considering *doing* it?"

Her mouth gaped open in confusion.

"I'm sitting here listening to the words coming out of my mouth and even *I* can't believe I'm asking this of you." I shook my head in self-disgust. "I can't believe I tried to make this work. I was so stupid. But I couldn't face losing you."

She stood in front of me, fear widening her eyes. "Don't do this, Joe. I *know* you. You don't want to do this."

"I'm not strong enough to fight them, Rose." I shook my head, trying to hold back my tears. I needed to get myself together and end this. My parents were too powerful and I couldn't risk hurting Rose any more than I already had. "You're the strong one. Not me."

"What are you talking about?" She grasped my hands, her nails digging into my skin. "That's not true, Joe. I've spent four months with you. I *know* you."

"No. You knew the me I so desperately wanted to be. A man free to live his life without family obligations. Free to love you."

"They're holding something over your head," she whispered. "That's why it took you so long last night. You were telling them *no thank you*, and they threw something bad at you to make sure you did what they said." Her eyes lit up with understanding. "It's about me."

I closed my eyes. I didn't want her to know the danger she was in. I was supposed to protect her, not put her in the position to be hurt. I'd failed her last night and I was failing her again.

"No more secrets, Joe. We can't make this work if we have secrets."

"You don't want to know," I pleaded with her. "Just let it go. Let *me* go."

"Let you go? No! We can fight this together."

"Rose, my parents are terrible people." Defeated, I rested my head in my hands. "It's not just about you and none of it's true. But the media doesn't care. They'll run with it, and no one pays any attention to retractions."

"What is it?"

"They've concocted some nonsense about Mike bribing county officials for his construction business."

Her face paled. "Oh, that's bad."

"They have photos of Violet with Brody McIntosh coming out of a motel. They plan to say they had an affair and left their spouses for each other."

"Oh, God." She looked like she was about to be sick. "What about me?"

"It's not true."

"I know. What is it?"

My head pounded. "My father has set up an account in your name, and he had someone postdate the opening for last May."

"Why would they do that?"

"He also postdated a money transfer for last May."

"I don't understand." Her voice rose in alarm.

"Rose, they transferred the money into one of Daniel Crocker's bank accounts. They set it up to make it look like you hired Crocker to kill your mother."

She looked like she was about to pass out so I sat in a chair and pulled her onto my lap. Anything to be close to her before I was forced to leave her. "I was gone so long because I begged and pleaded for them to not do this, not to take you away from me." I searched her face, tears burning my eyes. "You're the only good thing I've ever had in my life. *I want you.* You have no idea how much I *need* you." I paused, the pain of what I had to do nearly consuming me. "But I can't destroy you." I groaned and pressed my lips against hers. "Oh, God. I can't believe I even considered it." I pulled her against my chest, burying my face into her shoulder as I started to cry. "If I love you, I'll let you go."

Her head shook and she panicked. "No! I don't want you to let me go."

"If I don't, they'll destroy you. They've agreed for me to have a test engagement to see how the voters respond to you, but the things they expect you to do and not do will make you miserable. You'll end up resenting me for it. The life they expect me to live isn't you."

She grabbed my face. "But it's not you, either. Can you tell me that you'll be happy?"

"Rose, it doesn't matter if I'm happy. My parents don't care."

"But *I* care. I can't let you do this, Joe. I can't let you throw us away."

"Don't you see?" I pleaded. "If I don't run for this senate seat, my parents will ruin you. There won't be any *us* because you'll be in prison. Not to mention what they plan on doing to Violet and Mike."

She clung to my arms. "Then I'll do what I have to do to be with you. I'll follow their rules."

I smiled, but my heart wasn't in it. "You think you can pretend you don't know Neely Kate and live with it? You can ignore someone who needs help? It will eat you up inside. Why do you think I was so messed up before I met you?"

"Joe, there has to be a way!"

I leaned my forehead against hers, searching for the strength I needed. For once in my miserable life I had to think about someone else. I owed this to Rose. I couldn't protect her before, but I could do it now. Even if it meant sacrificing the only thing that I'd ever wanted. "I wish there was." I gave her a soft kiss. "This is the only thing I can do to protect you, and for once I'm man enough to do it. The irony is that I'm losing you in the process."

She waved her left hand at me, showing me her ring. "You asked me to marry you. That means something, Joe."

"Of course it means something. Losing you is like losing a part of myself." My voice cracked and I kissed her, knowing this was the last time I'd hold her and touch her. How did I go back to my empty life and live without her?

Rose was becoming more upset, and I knew I had to stop prolonging this torture. "No." I slid her off my lap and stood. "I'm just making this harder for both of us."

I went into her room and pulled a bag from the closet and began to stuff my clothes into it, trying to ignore her pathetic cries. Everything in me screamed to comfort her, but I couldn't.

Last week I was planning to move to Henryetta to live with her. Now I was leaving her. How could this be happening?

Rose stood in the doorway, but moved toward me. "Joe, *please.*" She reached for my hand to stop me, but I shook it off. I could barely make myself do this as it was. I forced myself to focus on what needed to be done and moved around her.

She stepped in front of me. "Joe, stop! *Please.* We can figure something out. We'll go somewhere together. We'll run away, go somewhere your parents will never find us."

Could we? Could we find somewhere that my parents could never find us? We could live in peace and raise a family, and I'd wake up every morning with her next to me and go to bed every night with her in my arms.

Rose held onto my neck and pressed herself against me. "We can go anywhere. How about we live on a beach where we can live in our swimsuits? Me half-naked all the time. You'd like that." She gave me her shy sexy smile, the one she flashed when she was trying to be sexy but worried she was making a fool of herself. Why hadn't I ever told her she didn't have a thing to be worried about?

My body reacted to hers, ignoring the orders from my brain, I closed my eyes, soaking her in.

She kissed me softly and instinct and despair kicked in. I wrapped my arms around her back, and pulled her closer, kissing her with pent-up frustration. I reached for the back of her neck, tilting her head back so I could deepen the kiss.

Her hands slid up, under my shirt, trailing up my back, and I held her tighter. I needed her closer. I couldn't let her go.

"I don't want to lose you, Joe."

I stopped, staring at her in horror. I was supposed to be leaving her, not making love to her. My hands dropped and I tried to back up out of her hold, but she refused to let go.

"You keep saying I'm the best thing that's ever happened to you. If that's true, then why aren't you fighting for me?"

My heart exploded, agony soaking into every cell in my body. She didn't know what was at stake. My own soul was already poisoned by my family. I couldn't let the same thing happen to her. "Don't you see that I am? I'm fighting so you don't lose *you*. If I let you become the person my mother wants you to be, not only will you resent me for it, but you will no longer be the woman I love." I tried to smile, to show her how much I loved her. "I don't *want* you to change." I gently pulled her arms from my back. "One day you'll thank me for this."

I turned around and grabbed my bag. I needed to leave now, before my resolve broke.

"What do you want from me, Joe?" she begged.

I stopped in front of her, the pain on her face nearly my undoing. She was the one person I'd give my life to protect and to keep from feeling even an ounce of pain, and here I was, not only stabbing her but twisting the knife even deeper.

I knew her. She'd hope this was a mistake. She'd hope that I'd come to my senses and come back to her. I had to make sure she really let me go. "I want you to move on with your life. I want you to be happy."

"*Happy*? How can you expect me to be happy without you?"

I knew that her happiness meant she'd be with another man. The thought nearly killed me, but for once I needed to think about someone else's well-being before my own. Especially Rose's. "Promise me you'll try."

She didn't answer, defiance flickering in her eyes before she reached for her ring, tugging it over her knuckle.

I put my hand over hers. "No. I don't want it back. I bought it for you, Rose. It's yours." I lifted her chin. "I want to look at you one last time."

"I'm bruised and swollen. I don't even have on makeup. *This* is how you want to remember me?"

She didn't even know how beautiful and special she was. I hoped to God when she found someone else he loved her as much as I did. But the thought of her loving someone else broke me, nearly making my knees buckle. I fought to keep from crying. "You're beautiful. Yes, this is how I want to remember you, just like this. Brave and strong and willing to stand up for what you believe in. Don't ever let anyone change you to be what they need. Me included, Rose." I kissed her gently, her soft lips against mine. Then I lifted my head and walked to the door.

"So that's it?" She followed me into the living room and she looked so broken it took everything within me not to go to her and hold her. "It's over, just like that?"

I opened the front door and stopped. I didn't think I could do this. If I really loved her, I'd do anything to protect her. Even if that meant setting her free. My damned parents had made sure of that. I was too stupid to see that they'd kill any chance at happiness that fell outside of their plan. "It was over from the beginning. I've just been waiting for my past to catch up to me." *Just one step out the door, Joe. If you love this woman, you will let her go.* Still I hesitated. Once I left it was over. "Goodbye, Rose."

I shut the door behind me as my world crashed around me. I was on autopilot as I opened the car door and tossed my bag into the back and got inside. I was halfway down the street before I realized I'd actually started the car and was driving. If I was this big of a mess, how was Rose handling it?

She was experiencing the biggest trauma of her life, and I wasn't there to comfort her. I couldn't stand the thought of her being alone and almost turned around to go back to her.

*No.*

Instead, I pulled out my cell phone and called Neely Kate.

"Joe, is Rose okay?" she sounded worried.

"No." I knew she was asking about her injuries from the night before, but I couldn't bring myself to clarify. My voice broke with my tears. I only needed to hold it together to get through this phone call. "She needs you, Neely Kate."

"I can get off at lunch."

Rose couldn't be alone that long. "No! She needs you *now*."

"Okay." She sounded scared, not that I blamed her. "I'll go now. Where is she?"

"She's home." I choked out. "Thank you." I ended the call before she could ask any more questions and held it together until I passed over the Fenton County line. Then I pulled the car over to the side of the road and leaned over the steering wheel and sobbed.

My heart irrevocably broken

# Part two

## Rose

# Chapter Six

Within a couple of hours after Joe left, I'd finally gotten myself somewhat together. And while I loved Neely Kate and Violet, I needed to be alone. All their hovering was making me claustrophobic.

My cell phone rang in the kitchen, and my heart lurched, the possibility of who might be on the other end catching my breath. Was it Joe? Had he called to tell me he'd changed his mind? But I couldn't make myself get up to answer it, scared my wavering hope would be defeated.

Neely Kate cast a wary glance at me before she went into the kitchen, returning to the doorway with the still-ringing cell in her hand. "It's Mason."

I sighed, trying not to cry with disappointment. With all the trauma of the morning, I'd forgotten I still had to go to the police department. "He's probably calling to tell me when to go give my statement."

Neely Kate answered. "Hey, Mason. It's Neely Kate." She paused and pointed to the phone with raised eyebrows.

I shook my head.

"She's busy at the moment. Can I take a message?" She kept her gaze on me while she listened for several seconds. "Okay, I'll bring her down at one." Her eyes widened. "*Where's Joe?*" She looked at me with raised eyebrows, wanting me to provide an answer to the question Mason must have asked.

I shook my head. I couldn't deal with answering more questions at the moment.

"Joe went back to El Dorado," Neely Kate said then cringed as Mason responded. "No, that's okay. I don't mind bringing her." She paused again. "Okay. I'll tell her." She hung up and leaned her head against the doorjamb. "Mason's going to bring you home. I couldn't think of any reason why he couldn't."

"That's okay." I sighed. "Thank you."

"You know he's going to find out sooner rather than later. He's going to take one look at you this afternoon and figure out that something's wrong."

"I know, but I'll deal with it then." I was about to cry again. "I need a shower or a bath. I'm still gross from last night."

Violet jumped up. "That's a good idea. A nice long bath is just what you need. I'll get it started for you."

"Thanks, Vi." I grabbed her hand and squeezed. "Why don't you go back to the nursery? I'm better now and there's nothing you can do, especially since I have to go to the police station. I'll call you after I give my statement."

Her mouth twisted in indecision. "I can come and sit with you."

The last thing Violet needed was to hear the horrific details of my kidnapping and almost murder. "I'll probably have to be alone when I talk to the police. Or Mason will be with me. I'll be fine."

She hesitated. "Okay, but why don't you come spend the night at my house tonight? Just like old times."

I nodded. "Sure." Old times. The last time I'd spent the night with Violet was months ago after we'd found out that

Momma wasn't my birthmother. But before Momma's murder—and before Joe—I used to spend at least one night a week at her house in an attempt to escape Momma's vicious tongue. "I'd like that."

She offered me a tight smile and rubbed my arm. "Good. It's settled. I'll pack a bag for you and bring it to the nursery. Neely Kate will take you to the station and Mason can bring you to the nursery when you're done. If you don't feel like hanging around, we can close early today."

I nodded.

She disappeared into the bathroom, and I heard the water start to run.

"Can I get you anything?" Neely Kate asked, still standing in the doorway. "Are you hungry or thirsty?"

"No, just tired."

"If you want, you can take a nap after your bath. I'll wake you up in time to go to the station."

"Don't you need to get back to work?"

She made a face. "Nah. Tiffany's got it under control. If I go back to work, I'll just worry about you."

"I'm fine now," I said, wiping my face. "See? I'm not sobbing uncontrollably anymore."

"You're still in shock, Rose. When this happened to me, I didn't want to be alone for days."

I teared up again but tried to smile. "Someone broke up with *you*? How stupid was *that guy*?"

"As stupid as Joe, apparently. But it obviously turned out to be a good thing for Ronnie."

I couldn't hold back my tears, and she pulled me into a hug. I hated that people were going to think so badly of Joe, especially when he did this to protect me and Violet. If it were just me, I'd take on his parents. I'd go to Mason and tell him everything and let him put Joe's parents in their place. But I couldn't risk exposing Violet. Even if she was the one to put herself in this position.

Neely Kate pulled back and looked into my eyes. "It's going to be okay, Rose. I promise. It's gonna hurt like hell for a bit, but you're gonna be okay."

I shook my head, trying to catch my breath. "My life is nothing without him. If it weren't for Joe, I'd still be scared of my own shadow."

Neely Kate scrunched her face in disgust. "Please, girl. Give yourself some credit. Sure, Joe helped encourage you and pushed you in a few directions you needed to go, but *you* were the one who started breaking out of your shell and becoming the person you are right now." She smiled, tears filling her eyes. "And you've only just started growing."

I leaned my cheek on her shoulder, still crying.

"I know right now it hurts like a railroad tie was shot through your gut, but you'll get through this and be happy again. I promise. Look at me. That other boy broke my heart but now I'm married to Ronnie, and I've never been happier."

I couldn't imagine how I could be happy again. I couldn't imagine any kind of life without Joe. The thought of trying ripped my wound open wide.

Violet emerged from the bathroom and pulled me away from Neely Kate. "Come on, Rose. Let's get you in the bath."

The water was still running into the tub, but the room was full of steam. Violet had put a fluffy towel on the closed toilet seat and hung my robe on a hook on the back of the closet door. She leaned over and turned off the water.

"I made it nice and hot, just like you like it so go ahead and get in. I've put a washrag on the side, along with some of that lavender soap you love."

"Thank you, Violet." My voice broke.

She grabbed the uninjured left side of my face. "It's gonna be okay, one day at a time, Rose. One minute at time if you have to. And I'll be here every step of the way. I won't let you go through this alone."

"Thanks."

Alone. That was my biggest fear. I'd lived most of my life feeling alone, ostracized from everyone and everything. Now that I'd had a taste of belonging to someone, I didn't want to go back to that loneliness again.

She closed the door and I stripped off Joe's shirt, the scent of him still lingering in the cotton. I started to cry again as I took off my shorts and stepped into the tub, sliding down into the bath. The warm, almost too hot, water soothed my aching muscles, but my head still throbbed from my stitches and my crying. I grabbed the washrag and cleaned the right side of my head as best I could without getting my stitches wet. When I finished, I leaned back, resting my neck on the folded towel Violet had left for me.

Logically, I knew I'd get over this. People broke up with each other every day and you didn't see them falling down and dying of unhappiness. But unhappiness didn't kill you that way. It was a slow malignancy that stole your hope. You didn't fall over dead, you faded away into nothingness.

I closed my eyes and thought about Joe. He was hurting too. He hadn't wanted to break up with me. I saw how much it killed him to walk out my door. How was he coping, especially when he had to go back to his campaign? At least I had people who loved me and would help me through this. Joe had no one.

I must have dozed off, because a soft rap on the door startled me.

The door opened a crack and Neely Kate's voice floated through the opening. "Rose?" She paused. "You've been in there a long time. Are you okay?"

"Yeah," I answered, but my voice sounded groggy.

"You've got about an hour before we have to leave. Do you want to get out and lie down for a little bit?"

I closed my eyes with a sigh. Life went on even when I didn't feel like moving on with it. "I'll be out in a minute."

"I know you weren't hungry, but I made you some lunch."

"Okay."

The door shut and I climbed out of the now cold water, my muscles aching in protest. I dried off and put on my robe before going into my bedroom. When I reached for my underwear drawer, the partially open drawer that I'd given Joe for his things made me draw in my breath. I pulled it open staring into the empty space.

He was really gone.

I pulled off Joe's ring and studied the diamonds. They weren't very big, and I suspected Joe could afford bigger, but he knew that I didn't wear gaudy things. The simpler the better. Tears filled my eyes, blurring the stones. Everything I'd been dreaming of the last few months was gone. Completely sucked away. Without Joe, what was left? I knew I was being shortsighted, but at that moment, I didn't care. I didn't want to think of a life without him.

But Joe was right, as hard as it was to admit. I would be miserable if I tried to live up to his parents' expectations. I tried to live up to Momma's and look how well that had turned out. The problem with attempting to live up to other people's expectations was that you were destined to fail before you even began. I had failed Momma and I would have failed Joe's parents too. Then I would have lost him anyway. I couldn't forget there was more at stake here. I couldn't risk hurting Violet.

There was no way to fix this.

With a sob, I dropped the ring into the empty drawer and pushed it shut. I'd only known Joe four months out of my twenty-four years. I *would* get over this. Eventually.

After I put on a pair of jeans and T-shirt, I found Neely Kate in the kitchen. "There wasn't much in your cabinets, but I found some soup. Besides, my grandma says nothing warms a broken heart like a hot bowl of soup."

I smiled up at her through a fresh batch of tears. "Thanks."

She placed a bowl in front of me as I sat down. She slid into the chair Joe sat in when he broke my heart and I blinked back tears. Would everything in my house remind me of him? When I added all the days I'd known him, he'd been here less than half of the time. So why was he so much a part of this house? So deeply embedded in my heart.

Neely Kate's gaze moved to my ring-less left hand, but she remained silent.

I could only get about half the bowl down before my stomach cramped, and I pushed the soup away. "I'm going to finish getting ready."

"Okay."

But when I stared at my reflection in the mirror, I realized putting on makeup was pointless. The right side of my face was bruised, and my eyes were swollen and bloodshot from crying. My hair was still dirty, despite my attempt to get the matted blood out. I was never going to look presentable. The Henryetta police were going to have to deal with looking at me.

On the way to the station, Neely Kate bantered on and on about her sister and her grandma, purposely avoiding anything that had to do with Ronnie. When she pulled into the lot, she turned off the engine and turned to me. "Are you sure you're okay with Mason taking you to the nursery? He's bound to ask questions about why you're so upset."

Why was I so worried about Mason finding out? I sighed. "He's going to notice that I've been crying, and I'll tell him. He's my friend so there's nothing for me to worry about. It's silly to *not* tell him." I smiled at her. "I just don't feel like answering a lot of questions, but it'll be fine."

"You can always call me if you change your mind. I'll come back and get you."

And I knew she would. She'd drop everything to help me. I leaned over and hugged her. "Thank you. I promise, if I need you, I'll call."

She walked inside the police station with me, and the anxiety I felt anytime I had to deal with the police crept up my spine. I took a deep breath as we entered the front door, telling myself that I had nothing to worry about. I hadn't done anything wrong. But the chaos and emotional upheaval of the morning only added to my anxiety.

After I checked in with the receptionist, she called Detective Taylor. He came up front, pausing in the doorway with a grim smile. "Come on back and I'll take your statement."

Neely Kate squeezed my hand before she left, and I followed the detective into the same room I'd given my statement after Jimmy DeWade had tried to strangle me months ago. I'd been worried about what the police would do with my statement, but I'd had Mason and Joe with me. A fresh pang of anxiety hit me as I looked around the room. This time I was alone.

"Where's Mason?" I asked as Taylor shut the door. "I thought he was going to be here."

He sat down, his face expressionless as he watched me. "He's running late so we're gonna start without him."

"I'd rather wait for Mason."

He crossed his legs and rested his forearm on the table. "How is it that you're so friendly with the assistant DA?"

I may have been upset about Joe, but Taylor's attitude lit a fire in my chest. "I don't see how my personal life is any of your business."

"It seems that your personal life is what got you in the position you're in right now."

"What exactly is *that* supposed to mean?"

His eyebrows rose. "You tell me."

I'd had a craptastic morning, and I refused to deal with this too. I stood. "I think we're done."

He leaned forward, anger darting from his eyes. "We're far from done, Ms. Gardner, so I suggest you sit down."

I moved to the end of the table, my hand on my hip. "Am I being held against my will?"

"Not at the moment."

I walked across the room and reached for the doorknob. "When Mason shows up, I'll give my statement. Until then, I'm gonna wait out in the lobby." I pulled the door open ready to storm out, but came face to face with Mason, nearly bumping into him.

He grabbed my arm, his eyes wide with surprise. "Rose, are you leaving already?"

To my irritation, my eyes burned and my voice shook. "Can I give my statement to someone else?"

Confusion wrinkled his brow as he looked over his shoulder. "Why? What happened?"

"Detective Taylor's suggesting I brought the attack upon myself."

Mason's face darkened. "Taylor, is that correct?"

"Deveraux, I assure you that she misunderstood me." Taylor answered in his easy-going, good-ol'-boy voice. "You know how sensitive women can be."

Mason's gaze shifted to my face.

I could have made a big deal of it and probably should have, but I just wanted to go home. I closed my eyes. "Let's get this over with."

I walked back into the room and sat in the chair. Taylor's mouth lifted into a slight grin of triumph.

What had I ever done to get on his bad list? Back when I was on Bruce Wayne's jury, Neely Kate had suggested that the police didn't like me because I'd made them look incompetent by proving I hadn't murdered Momma. I suspected that she was right.

Mason sat in a chair next to me and listened while I gave my statement, every so often shooting angry looks at Taylor as he asked questions. With Mason in the room, Taylor's attitude improved, but I still sensed an undercurrent of contempt. When we finished, Mason stood, keeping his eyes on the detective. "Rose, will you wait in the hall? I need to talk to Detective Taylor for a moment."

"Sure." I said, casting a glance to both men before I walked out into the hall.

Within a second of my shutting the door, I heard Mason's muffled voice in angry snippets. "If you *ever*...I'll make sure you...*Have I made myself clear?*"

Thirty seconds later he emerged from the room, anger rolling off of him until he saw me. The hard lines of his face softened and he put an arm around my back. "I'll take you home now."

I shot a look back into the room. Taylor's face was so red he looked like he was about to have a stroke.

Mason kept his arm around me as we walked out of the station in silence, all eyes in the station on both of us. When we reached his car, he opened the door for me and drew in a breath. "Jonah's mother, Wanda Pruitt—otherwise known as Rhonda Bellamy—is being held on a hundred thousand dollars bond. After talking to Jonah this morning, I suspect he won't put up the money to bail her out, even if he had the money to do so." His hand rested on my shoulder as he looked into my eyes. "Rose, I want you to know she won't be able to hurt you again. And if by some miracle she comes up with the bail money, I'll be sure to let you know as soon as I know it."

"Will you be trying her case?"

"No, not since I was personally involved in her apprehension. The DA will be prosecuting her."

"Oh." I couldn't imagine the pain Jonah was going through after finding out what his mother had done. "How's Jonah doing?"

"He's still in the hospital, but he'll probably get out tomorrow. He's pretty upset about his mother, but he's got plenty of the older women who are under his spell waiting outside his door, eager to help him when he gets home."

"I found out why all the older woman love him so much. He told me yesterday." Everything from the day before seemed like it happened weeks ago.

Mason's eyes widened in surprise. "Did you now?"

"It's because he spends time with them. They're just lonely old women who need someone to talk to. Jonah likes their cooking and they like his company. Nothing suspicious there." I dropped my gaze, unable to look at Mason. The older women's loneliness only reminded me of my own.

"Well, thank you for setting the record straight."

I nodded, not trusting myself to speak.

"I've dealt with Taylor, but you need to let me know if he upsets you again."

I closed my eyes and leaned against the car. "You didn't have to do that, Mason. Now he'll hate me even more."

"If you think I'm going to stand back and let him treat you disrespectfully, then you don't know me very well at all," he said, his voice hard.

I opened my eyes. "I *do* know you, Mason. That's why I said it. I don't want you to get into trouble because of me."

A soft smile lifted his mouth. "Don't worry about me. I'm perfectly capable of taking care of myself."

"And so am I."

Pride filled his eyes. "You've proved that time and time again, Rose, but it doesn't mean I can't intervene on your behalf when I feel the need."

Joe said he'd take care of me and where was he now? I spun and slid into the front seat, trying to keep my tears at bay. Was there no end to my tears?

Mason shut my door then came around and climbed behind the wheel. "Do you want me to take you home?"

"No, to the nursery."

"You're working today?" He sounded surprised. "Aren't you supposed to be recuperating?"

"I'm just working this afternoon, I need to do something." As I said the words, I realized how true they were. I needed to feel the potting soil in my hands. I needed to be anywhere but home where memories of Joe lingered everywhere.

Mason was silent a moment. "So, Joe went back to El Dorado?"

I looked out the side window. "Yeah."

"Is he still on his undercover assignment?"

"No, he decided to run in the senate race." I was proud my voice didn't tremble.

After a couple of seconds, Mason's soft voice broke the silence. "Rose, are you okay?"

He sounded so concerned that I couldn't stop a fresh batch of tears from rolling down my cheeks. "No."

Without a word, he turned into the parking lot of the hardware store, parking his car in the empty back lot. "What happened?"

I took a breath. "Joe and I broke up this morning."

He was silent for several seconds. "I'm sorry."

"You're not going to ask why?"

"I already suspected. You'll tell me if you want me to know."

I sniffed. "How did you know we broke up?"

"Your ring is missing and you're clearly upset."

"You wanna know the funny part?" I asked, turning toward him.

His eyes were full of support and he grimaced. "What?"

"I was wearing his ring, but I never even accepted his proposal."

"So *you* broke it off?"

I pressed my lips together. "No. He did. But we both agreed that I'd make a terrible senator's wife."

"I'm sorry."

I released a soft cry, and he pulled me into a hug, resting my cheek on his shoulder. We stayed there for several minutes, one of his hands rubbing soft circles on my back.

"I feel so stupid," I finally said.

He pulled back, staring into my face. "What on earth *for?*"

"For crying on you two days in a row. You're going to think I'm nothing but a big crybaby." I rubbed the wet spot on his shoulder. "Now I owe you for the cleaning of *two* shirts."

He pulled my hand off of his shoulder and cradled it between both of his palms in his lap. "Rose, you know I'm here for you when you need me."

"I know. Thank you." While I knew he was, I wasn't exactly sure *why* he was. Was it because he was genuinely my friend, or because he had feelings for me? Or a combination of both? I was too tired and emotionally drained to think about it too much. But I also noticed something else. While there was concern in his eyes, there was no pity. "And thank you for not looking at me like I'm pathetic."

"Rose," he hesitated, conflict brewing in his hazel eyes. They seemed greener than usual today. "You are *far* from pathetic. I know how much you care about Joe, and I know you're hurting, and I'm sorry for that. I'm sorry you have to go through even more pain than you already have these last few months." He shifted in his seat. "But you're strong and you'll get through this. You don't deserve pity. If anyone does, it's Joe."

My eyes widened in panic, my breath catching in my throat. Why did he feel sorry for Joe? "You know about Joe's parents?" Who else knew?

"*Of course* I know Joe's parents had something to do with this. But it's probably better that you found out now how easily Joe is manipulated by them, before it was too late. Think about it this way: you've got entire life ahead of you, full of possibilities, even if you don't want to consider them now. The only thing Joe has to look forward to is a life full of manipulation."

My shoulders sagged in relief. Mason didn't know about the blackmail. If I were honest with myself, no matter how hard it was to admit, I couldn't help thinking Mason was right. I suspected Joe had spent the last few months hiding from his parents because he wasn't strong enough to stand up to them.

Or maybe he knew what they were capable of doing to get their way, and he'd hid to put it off as long as possible. Either way, he was stuck under their thumb. When Momma died, I'd been freed.

Joe and I were more alike than I realized. Only I'd finally escaped from my life of being controlled, and Joe was still imprisoned.

I offered Mason a soft smile. "Thanks."

"For what?"

"For helping me put things in perspective. You're always good at that."

He grinned. "That's what I'm good for—perspective and shirts to cry on."

I couldn't hide the smile that tugged at my lips. "And putting police detectives in their place."

An ornery grin lit up his face. "That's a freebie. I love to do that one any chance I get."

I laughed softly, feeling a little bit better, even if for only a few seconds.

His voice turned serious. "You know I'm here if you need anything."

"Thanks, I do." And I did. He'd proven it time and time again. I could always count on Mason.

He dropped my hand and shifted the car into drive. "To the nursery?"

"Yeah."

We didn't talk the rest of the way, but our silence was comforting instead of uncomfortable. When he parked in the nursery parking lot, he came around and opened my door then pulled me into a hug.

"Call me if you need me for anything," he whispered into my ear, then he got back in his car and drove away.

# Chapter Seven

Violet fussed over me when I walked through the front door of the shop. How did the statement go? Was I hungry or thirsty? Was I tired? Did I need to lie down?

After a few minutes, I couldn't take it anymore. "Violet, talking to Mason helped me feel better. What I really want to do is go in the backroom and work."

Her brow wrinkled. "Mason?" She paused, cocking her head. "What did *he* say?"

I wasn't sure why, but I felt the need to keep most of our conversation to myself. Maybe it was because I still didn't feel like I could trust her after I found out that she'd let the entire town think I'd stolen her inheritance.

Violet's betrayal cut me to the core. Especially when I thought of the sacrifice I was making to keep her affair with Brody a secret. But she was my sister. Revealing her secret wasn't an option. "Mason told me not to worry. That everything would work out in the end."

She put her hand on her hip and frowned. "But that's what I said."

She was right, but her comfort didn't have the same effect it had months ago. "Do we have any flower pots that need to be made?"

"Yeah." Violet didn't look happy that I changed the topic, but she must have given me a pass because of my emotional turmoil. "We're completely out of the pots with mums, straw grass, and asparagus ferns. Those have been a huge hit."

I headed to the back and spent the next two hours planting ten containers of flowers. The muscles of my back ached around my bruises, but it was worth the pain. The dirt and plants were my happy place, the one place where I belonged. When I worked with soil and flowers I was neither alone nor unhappy. I simply was.

As I was finishing the last pot, Violet poked her head in the back. "How are you doing?"

I looked up, startled out of my solitude. "Oh, fine."

"I'm sorry I haven't checked on you sooner. We had a sudden rush of customers." She paused. "Most of them were looking for you."

"Me? Why?"

"They've heard about you getting beat up by Miss Rhonda and they wanted to see you for themselves."

I scowled my disapproval, although I wasn't sure why I was surprised. "Sorry to disappoint them."

Violet's mouth twisted into an ornery grin. "We've gotten quite a few sales from it, even though I told them you weren't here so it worked out for *us*." She moved closer to me and lifted my chin. "You might want to hide out for a few more days. You look worse than the time you tangled with Daniel Crocker."

After Daniel Crocker had attacked me months ago, I'd gone back to work at the DMV because I was out of vacation days. I had the luxury of staying home now, but being here was the best place for me. I hadn't been an emotional mess the last couple of hours.

Violet closed up the shop while I cleaned up the potting table. When we walked through her front door, my niece and nephew threw their arms around my legs, squealing with excitement.

"Be careful!" Violet protested. "Aunt Rose is pretty sore."

But I didn't mind. I pulled them both into a hug, tears stinging my eyes again.

Violet's mother-in-law, Sheila, had been watching the children and she frowned her concern when she saw my bruised face.

"Rose is going to stay with us for a few days," Violet said under her breath.

Sheila nodded and the two women whispered in a huddle as I walked through the house, eager to see my little dog.

Ashley followed, jumping up and down. "Muffy's in the backyard."

As soon as I stepped onto the deck, Muffy ran toward me, jumping up in excitement. I squatted and rubbed her head, forcing back my rising tears. Even Muffy reminded me of Joe.

I wanted to lie down and cry. How could I go on without him?

"Why are you so sad, Aunt Rose?" Ashley asked, staring at me with large round eyes.

She caught me by surprise, and I fumbled with what to tell her. "Because Joe went away, and I don't know when I'll see him again."

"Are you and Joe getting a divorce like Momma and Daddy?"

"Oh." I gasped at her bluntness. "Yeah. I guess it's kind of like a divorce."

She threw her arms around my neck, her sweet scent of strawberry shampoo filling my nose. "I miss my Daddy, but I still get to see him. Maybe you can still see Joe."

I kissed her temple, wishing it were that simple. As far as I knew, I'd never see Joe again. The pain accompanying that thought was crippling.

The rest of the night was a blur as I went through the motions of eating dinner and helping Ashley with her kindergarten homework. I offered to give the kids a bath, happy for the distraction. Violet folded laundry, then disappeared into her room and closed the door for ten minutes. I glanced at it as I carried Mikey into his room to put on his diaper and pajamas.

"She hides in there sometimes," Ashley murmured when she saw me staring at the door. "She's talking to her friend."

My brow lowered. I had a feeling I knew who her friend was. "Do you tell your daddy that your mommy talks to a friend?"

Her head bobbed up and down. "He asks me when I visit him."

My anger rose and I tried to squash it down so Ashley didn't see it. One, I was angry with Mike for questioning his five-year-old daughter about his wife's behavior, but I was more angry with Violet because I knew who she was talking to. She'd told me the night before that she'd cut things off with Brody since Mike suspected she'd had an affair. Now it looked like she lied.

But I told myself that she could be talking to anyone about anything. She might have shut the door because she was talking about me. But I knew she wasn't.

The guilt on her face gave her away when she emerged from her room and stood in the bathroom doorway as I helped Mikey brush his teeth. "Ash and Mikey, tell Aunt Rose thank you for helping you get ready for bed."

"Thank you, Aunt Rose," Ashley said, hugging my leg.

Violet tucked her children into bed and I turned my back and left the room, tears stinging my eyes again. Less than a week ago, Joe and I had talked about children. Now that dream was gone too.

He'd left me less than twelve hours ago, but I missed him with an ache that consumed me. I grabbed my cell phone out of my purse, desperate to talk to him, my heart leaping when I saw that I had a text. But I stared at the lone message on my screen, my hope fading. The message was from Mason.

*You are stronger than you think.*

Was I? I'd survived so much in the last few months, but I'd had Joe by my side to help me. Now he was gone.

I covered my mouth to quiet my sob. Violet found me on the back deck minutes later, my shoulders shaking from my tears. She sat next to me and wrapped an arm around my back and pulled my head to her chest. I sank into her and cried, my anger at her fading as the familiarity of the past rushed back in. Violet had been the one to hold me after Momma's many punishments when I was little, often rocking me to sleep. Despite her many faults, Violet loved me. She'd been there for me years ago when no one else had. And she was here now.

Just like old times.

# Joe

# Chapter Eight

B y the time I'd pulled into the parking lot of the campaign headquarters, I'd gotten myself together as best I could. I walked into the strip mall office at 10:59 still wearing my sunglasses to hide my bloodshot eyes. My head aching as though someone had taken a baseball bat to it. Four eager college-aged kids—all of whom I was sure were handpicked by my father—sat at metal desks in the center of the room, looking up from their laptops as I walked past to the round tables at the back of the room. A *Joe Simmons for Arkansas Senate* vinyl sign hung on the back wall.

The bastard sat at one of the tables with a man I didn't recognize. "Joe," my father shouted. "Get over here. We have business to discuss."

I swallowed my bitterness, but it burned as it lodged in the pit of my stomach.

My father stood and gestured toward the unfamiliar man. "Joe, meet Teddy Bowman, your campaign manager. He'll be your new best friend over the next month or so."

Teddy rose, eyeing me up and down as he extended his hand. "Joe, nice to meet you."

I grabbed his hand and shook. Teddy couldn't be much older than me, but there was a hint of cynicism in his eyes, and I knew a patronizing tone when I heard one.

"I hope you're ready to hit the ground running." He grinned, but it looked calculated and carefully controlled. I was sure most people wouldn't see it, but I'd spent the last several years honing my judgment of people. My life had depended on it before. My sanity depended on it now.

My brow rose slightly and I smirked, taking off my sunglasses. "That's what my father tells me."

Teddy didn't look happy with my answer, but he sat down and examined his notes on the legal pad in front of him. "Your father says you recently became engaged."

I had expected Rose to come up for discussion, but I wasn't prepared for the kick in the gut that came with it. I let a moment pass before I stiffened my shoulders and answered. "Not anymore."

Triumph lit up my father's face. "That's not true, Joe."

I was too exhausted and heartbroken to play my father's games. I leaned back in my chair and rubbed my eyes. "What in the hell are you talking about? I broke up with Rose about an hour ago no thanks to you and Mom. I'm sure you're both *very* happy now."

My father scowled, shooting me a glare that assured me that he thought I was an incompetent fool. "Not Rose. Hilary."

"*Hilary?*"

He crossed his legs, folding his hands on his raised knee. "Yes, Hilary. Teddy agrees with your mother's suggestion. You need a wife or at least a fiancée to win this election."

"You've got to be kidding me?" I stood, my voice rising. "You think I'm going to break up with Rose and ask Hilary to *marry* me? Have you lost your mind?"

"Joe, control yourself!" my father shouted. "When are you going to grow up and use the balls God gave you?"

"If I used my balls, I'd walk out that front door right now!"

Dad banged his fist on the table, his face red. "That will be enough!"

Teddy's fingers rapped a rhythm on the table. "Are you two done now? Or will this go on long enough for me to run over to the Subway next door and get a footlong?" He asked with a bored expression on his face.

My father turned his rage on Teddy, shaking his finger across the table. "No one talks to me that way! I *hired* you, and I can fire your ass at any minute."

Teddy didn't look impressed. "Then do it because if I can't tell you like it is during this campaign, I might as well walk out the door right this minute and save us all a lot of time."

Dad's mouth clamped shut.

"Okay then." Teddy leaned forward and turned his blank gaze on me. "Joe, your father's right. You have a better chance of building a snowman in the Sahara than you do of beating Frank Delany as a single, unattached man."

"I don't give a damn about beating Frank Delany."

Teddy's eyes hardened. "I'll let you get away with a lot of things, and with your daddy's income at my disposal, I can clean up a lot of messes. We've got about a month to take you from being a nobody to winning this thing, but you've got to be all in, otherwise you're just wasting my time." His eyes narrowed. "And nothing pisses me off more than having my time wasted."

"You better think about your answer," Dad growled. "People are depending on it."

The implied threat was all too clear. *Damn him.* Gritting my teeth, I turned to stare out the window. "I'm in."

"Good," Teddy said, but he still sounded bored. "Tomorrow noon is the deadline to file your paperwork for the senate race. We could just send up the paperwork with a courier, but I think we should make a big splash with it, get some media coverage. We'll have you go up to Little Rock and file the paperwork yourself then hold a press conference on the steps of the capital building, announcing your candidacy with Hilary at your side, gazing at you like a dutiful bride-to-be."

I started coughing. "Have you seen Hilary? I doubt she's capable of looking dutiful, much less actually obeying an order."

"She'll toe-the-line," Dad bellowed.

Teddy placed his palm on the table. "That's settled then. We'll be in Little Rock by ten to file the paperwork, and I'll schedule a news conference to officially announce your candidacy." He flipped a page of his legal pad. "Given the fact you've lived in Little Rock as a state police detective, we'll play up your fight against crime. You'll look like a real life Batman—a young, good-looking crime fighter, with his attractive fiancée at his side." He turned to look at Dad. "She *is* attractive, isn't she?"

"She most certainly is."

"I'm not marrying her." He could make me break up with Rose, but there was no way in hell he could force me to marry someone I couldn't stand.

"Fine." Teddy turned to me with his condescending stare. "No one said you had to go through with marrying her. Just be engaged to her during the campaign and then break it off when the election's over, although I confess, it would be better to breakup after the state of the state address."

I shook my head in disgust.

"Even if you marry her, you wouldn't be the first to have a political marriage."

A political marriage? Before Rose, I probably would have accepted it. In fact, I was destined for it. But after Rose, I couldn't imagine the life sentence. I'd rather be miserably alone the rest of my life than in a marriage with Hilary.

Teddy shifted his weight. "I don't care if you marry her or not. Not right now. All I need you to do is tell the voters you're engaged and pretend you like the woman. Will that be too difficult for you?"

"No," My father barked in response. "He'll do it."

"With all due respect, J.R.," Teddy said dryly. "I need to hear this from Joe."

Could I pretend to like the bitch who had done everything in her power to hurt me? No. But I looked into my father's hardened face and thought about what he held over my head. His plan was ingenious and I never should have expected less. All he had to do was wait for me to find something I cared about so he could dangle it in front of me, threatening to destroy it. My father and Mason Deveraux were more alike than I cared to admit. Both men knew what they wanted and were willing to bide their time to get it.

"Yes," I grunted.

"Good, now we need to talk about your platform." Teddy shuffled his papers. "Our best bet jumping in this late to the campaign is to focus on your state police career and apply it to crime. We'll make you a pro-family, anti-violence Republican who personally did his part to keep Arkansas safe from the bad guys out to get its fragile citizens. I'm working on getting an endorsement from Huckabee."

We discussed the platform and my travel schedule with Teddy stopping to make phone calls and texts every few minutes. After his last phone call, he looked up grinning. "We're all set for the press conference tomorrow. You need to make sure your fiancée will be there."

"She'll be there," my father said. "She's taking a leave of absence from her position with the state police to work on the campaign."

That was news to me, but I wasn't surprised my father had set that in motion. After the disastrous dinner at their house, my parents had to know that Rose would never accept their conditions. But then, that had probably been their plan all along.

Teddy's gaze swung from me to my father. "Tell her to dress feminine—a dress, ruffles, maybe even pearls. We need to soften her for the older female voters and make her more traditional. Some of the older women will be turned off that she was in the state police. But if she dresses more like June Clever, we have a better shot. While she'll be the doting wife to Joe, she'll need a platform of her own, but minimized since this is only a state senate position. She'll have no real power yet, but will gain it as Joe advances through the political system. It would help if her focus remains consistent."

"She has one," Dad said. "She wants to focus on women and families affected by domestic violence."

My stomach revolted, and I swallowed to keep myself from flying apart. "You mean like she went out of her way to protect Savannah?"

My father's eyes narrowed, and his face reddened. "*Joseph.*"

For the first time in hours, Teddy showed some interest in our conversation. "Who's Savannah?"

"She's no one," Dad growled.

Teddy glanced back and forth between us. "No, she's definitely *someone*. Who is she?"

My father grunted his annoyance. "She was Joe's fling in Little Rock. He broke up with her and within a month she was pursued by a stalker and killed in her home. It was an unfortunate incident that had a profound effect on Hilary."

A profound effect on Hilary? I could have forgiven Hilary if she had shown even an ounce of remorse. Instead, she insisted that she was blameless of the entire situation.

Teddy's eyes focused on me, his face expressionless. "Who broke up with whom?"

I didn't want to get into this, but I was the one who had opened this can of worms. "I broke up with her."

"Did you have anything to do with her death?"

Did I? I'd asked myself that question more times than I could count. On one hand, I could claim myself inculpable. I hadn't stalked and killed her. But when I was honest with myself, I knew I'd played a part. I'd taken away the protection she needed with my cynicism and selfishness. There was no denying Savannah would have had a better chance of surviving if the Little Rock Police had believed her. Hilary had poisoned them and me into ignoring Savannah's cry for help. And for that, I would never forgive her. But the fact remained that I had my own share of responsibility in her death.

But I couldn't tell Teddy that. I couldn't tell anyone. My father had buried it deep under the stench of the multiple incidents I'd gotten myself into over the last eight years. And that was where it had to stay.

My jaw clenched. "No. She called me the night of her death and told me someone was outside her apartment. I told her to call the police. Hours later, she called me again, clearly upset saying that someone was in her apartment. I went over to check on her and found her dying from multiple stab wounds."

Teddy's eyes lit up. "So you're a hero."

"No," I snorted, looking away. "I'm far from a hero. I didn't get there in time. She died before the ambulance arrived."

"But we can use this." Excitement filled Teddy's voice as he grabbed his notebook and pen. "We can paint you as a hero who tried to—"

"*No*." I glared at my father. "I will *not* use her. That is non-negotiable."

For the first time since this mess began, my father's face softened. "All right, Joe. It's not on the table."

"Thank you." I swallowed the lump in my throat.

Dad turned toward Teddy. "You'd be better off using his big undercover bust in Henryetta a few months ago. He single-handedly took down a statewide crime ring in Fenton County, resulting with the arrest of Daniel Crocker."

I closed my eyes. "It wasn't single-handed."

"True, an informant who was part of the bust was killed, but he died a hero after he provided valuable information. But after the case was compromised with his death, Joe stepped up and got what the state police needed to make a bust."

I shook my head in disbelief. "You seriously want to use this case?"

"It's your biggest bust to date."

"Since when have you paid attention to my case record?"

"I've always paid attention."

That didn't surprise me, but my father had never approved of my decision to join the state police, and he'd sure never let on that he knew about what I was up to. But he made it his business to know everything. "It wasn't single-handed. I'd be dead if it weren't for Rose."

Teddy's eyebrows rose. "It takes two hours to find out that you're not the boring stuffed-shirt I thought you were. Why do I think there's more to this story? Who's Rose?"

"She's a civilian," my father said. "Crocker and the state police thought Ms. Gardner was an anonymous informant, but it was based on circumstantial evidence. Still, she got sucked into the case and her life was threatened. And Joe is being modest. It was Joe that saved Rose."

"Is this Rose the same Rose you are no longer engaged to?"

I swallowed. "We were never engaged."

"But you had a relationship?"

I blinked and looked out the window. I refused to break down in front of my father and let him gloat in my misery. "Yes. I met her during the case. I've been seeing her since."

"Until you recently broke up?"

I didn't answer.

Teddy grinned. "This is big. We can use this."

"I don't want to use it at all." There was no way I could talk about that case without the aching reminder of Rose. "I want to leave Rose out of this."

"Sounds like you've had a complicated love life." Teddy wrote down some notes. "How many of these complications could complicate your campaign?"

"None." My father pushed his chair back and leaned his arm on the table. "I've made sure of it."

Teddy grunted. "Let's hope you have. We don't have time to sort out a scandal and salvage the campaign should one of your complications jump up and bite you in the ass."

He showed me a schedule that included something every day with multiple town hall meetings coordinated in multiple towns and a few debates scheduled toward the middle and end of the campaign. "We'll let you get your feet wet before we throw you to the proverbial wolf."

By late afternoon, I was exhausted and Teddy noticed. "Go home, get a goodnight's sleep and plan on meeting me at the capital outside the secretary of state's office at 9:45. And bring your fiancée with you." Teddy gathered his papers and stood. "You've got the looks. You've got the background.

You've got potential appeal, but I'll be honest," He stuffed his papers into his bag and studied me. "At the moment you lack the charisma. You better pull some out of your ass by tomorrow or you'll be done before you even begin."

Over before I begin. The story of my life.

Without saying a word, I stood and headed for the exit. My father called my name, but I ignored him, needing the solitude of my car. I drove to my parents' house on autopilot. I walked through the front door and climbed the massive staircase to my old room, ignoring my mother's welcome call from the living room. I shut the door behind me and sat in my old navy and cream plaid overstuffed chair, staring out the window at storm clouds brewing in the distance.

My gaze shifted to a trophy on my old desk. I'd won it the first summer that I'd attended the young leader's summer camp. The one Hilary had mentioned the night before. "Most Promising Rising Political Leader" was engraved on the front. Funny how it had filled my heart with a dread now that was equal to the dread I felt the day I'd won it. This damn award had sealed my political fate, and I was smart enough to realize it when the counselor had placed it in my hand. Even at the age of ten.

But my fate had been sealed before that summer, just as my father had admitted the night before. I'd been born to run for political office. Refusing this path had never been an option.

I glanced around the room that I grew up in. Little had changed over the years. My mother had had the room professionally decorated in the baseball theme when I was five. Ornate paneling covered the walls up to a chair rail with navy wallpaper with baseballs above it and a navy bedspread covered the full-sized bed with a heavy wooden headboard. The room looked like it had come out of a magazine, but I never felt like I belonged here. Something had always been missing in my life, and I'd finally found her a few short months ago.

I wasn't sure how I could go on without Rose. I wasn't sure I even wanted to try.

I'd only left her hours ago, and we'd spent over half of our relationship apart, but the finality of never seeing her again filled me with overwhelming despair.

Tears burned my eyes, and I leaned my temple into the cushions of the chair. What was the point of any of this without her?

A knock on the door got my attention, and my mother entered the room.

Her face softened when she saw me, moving to the side of my old bed and sitting on the edge. "I take it Rose didn't agree."

I refused to answer, not that I could with the lump in my throat.

"It's better to find out now before your heart was broken."

I snorted. Before my heart was broken. What in the hell did she think I was upset about now?

"I understand this is difficult for you, Joe. But I promise you that time does heal all wounds. And one day, you will agree that this all worked out for the best."

I stared at the tree branches outside my window.

She was silent for a moment. "We have guests tonight. Several couples who wish to contribute to your campaign, so you'll need to dress for dinner."

I still didn't answer. I was the puppet and they were pulling the strings. Nothing had really changed. Sure, different time, different circumstances, but I was still theirs to manipulate. Only this time, they were certain I would comply.

She stood and moved toward me, her fingers curling around my shoulder. "I know this hurts now, Joe, but I promise it will get easier." She paused, a hint of sadness creeping into her voice. "Not necessarily better, but it will get easier once you accept your fate."

I looked up at her in surprise.

"We all have our purpose in this world, and it's not always what we want it to be. Despite what our heart wants." Her eyes clouded then she gave me a stiff smile. "A tuxedo isn't necessary tonight. A suit and tie will be sufficient. Drinks begin at seven. Dinner at eight. I suggest you make an appearance at seven or soon after." She moved to the door and stopped. "Hilary will be in attendance. It's time for you to accept your full responsibility."

The door closed behind her. I picked up the trophy and stared it for a moment before throwing it against the wall.

A few hours later, I descended the staircase, arriving at the entrance of the living room full of guests promptly at seven.

Hilary stood across the room, talking to an older couple, her melodious laugh filling the room. She wore a tailored dress and heels, her hair pulled back at the sides. I paused in the entrance, searching for the gumption to go through with this. She pivoted, a smile spreading across her face as she saw me. Softness exuded from her. Her dress and the way she wore her hair reminded me of when we were younger, back when we were both innocent and unjaded. Hilary moved toward me, practically floating through the room until she reached me. Her beauty and her grace caught the attention of the other guests. The unabashed love on her face as she kept her gaze on me made it appear that she thought we were the only two people in the room.

Hilary always knew how to get attention.

She stopped in front of me and pressed a kiss on my cheek. "You can do this, Joe. You've spent your entire life preparing for this."

I looked down at her face, numb inside.

"We'll get through this. Together." She slipped her hand in mine, pulling me into the room.

Years of instinct and practice from working undercover kicked in.

Showtime.

The corners of my mouth lifted into a smile my heart didn't feel like giving, and I greeted the first couple I came to, offering my hand. "Hi. I'm Joe Simmons and I'd like your support for the Arkansas State Senate."

# Part Three

## Joe

# Chapter Nine

*Two weeks later*

I looked out the window of the motel room, twisting a glass in my hand.

My father stood behind me, delivering a monologue that had turned into a nonsensical mash of words in my inebriated state. I tried to read the motel sign in the parking lot to jog my memory. What town was I in? I'd lost track days ago.

"Did you hear me?" his voice broke through my muddled thoughts.

I blinked, keeping my gaze out the window. "Hear what?"

"Have you heard a damned thing I've said?"

My hand tightened around the glass, the ice cubes clicking against the sides. "No."

He cursed for several seconds. "And that attitude is exactly why you're losing in the polls, Joe. You have to step up your game."

*Step up my game.* That meant I had to actually give a damn, which I didn't. "Fine."

"Have you even prepared for this town hall meeting in Preston?"

Preston. So that's where we were, not that it really mattered. These meetings were all the same. I shrugged. "What's there to prepare for? I'll pull out the Joe Simmons charm and have the votes of women age eighteen to fifty all tied up and in the bag."

"That's not going to work in Preston. You'll be facing a group of irate farmers wanting to know what kind of subsidies you're going to vote for once you get into office."

"So answer this two-part question for me, Dad." I turned to face him with a sneer. "One, what subsidies will I promise them, and two, what subsidies will I actually vote for? Because, obviously this is your dog-and-pony show. I'm just the front man."

A low growl rumbled from his chest. "You need to act like you give a damn, Joe."

"See?" I turned and held out my glass toward him, extending a wavering finger. "*That* was where you screwed up. You should have made sure I actually gave a damn in the first place."

His eyes hardened. "Have you been drinking all afternoon?"

I gave him an ugly smile, holding out my glass. "Guilty as charged."

His face reddened, and he looked like he was about to have a stroke. As if I could be so lucky. "What the hell are you thinking?"

"I'm thinking I can't face another freaking day on the campaign trail with Daddy Dearest without fortification."

"*How drunk are you?*"

"Not drunk enough."

My father stomped over and jerked the drink from my hand. "Have you really reverted to frat behavior?"

I reached for the glass, but he jerked it out of my reach, not difficult given my poor coordination. "That insinuates I actually *partook* in frat behavior. I was too busy studying to get good enough grades to get into Vanderbilt law school."

"And then you didn't even go there!" His voice boomed throughout the room.

I offered him my best smart-assed grin. "And *there's* the burn. I got into Vanderbilt and I didn't go. Score one for Joe."

His eyes narrowed. "Do you *really* want to go on this trip down Memory Lane? You paint yourself as a martyr when you were an undergrad, but you sure as hell made up for it when you started law school in Little Rock. I can start listing your transgressions if you like, but it might take *quite* some time."

My face heated with anger. "Why the hell not? Let's go for broke, right here in some piss-ant motel in some hell-hole town. Let's just get it all out in the open. Why don't I invite some reporters in here to get the scoop too?"

That seemed to get his attention. He stiffened then set my glass on the bathroom counter. "You're months shy of your thirtieth birthday, Joseph. Is it too much to ask you to act your age?"

"Is it too much to ask you to actually love me for me instead of my political potential?" The alcohol had loosened my tongue, and the words were out before I could stop them, but I was still sober enough to instantly regret it. As a young child, I'd learned to not show any sign of weakness to my father or he would use it against me. I'd be revisited by that gem, whether it be now or later.

Over the last few weeks, while I'd had plenty of time to wallow in my misery, I realized *that* was where I had screwed up so royally.

I'd let my parents know that I actually loved someone.

I thought my mother, who had begun to lament the fact she was never going to be a grandmother, would be thrilled that there were grandbabies on the horizon. I was too blind to admit they'd never approve of Rose. But then, I thought Rose would win them over—how could anyone meet Rose and not love her? I should have known they would never accept anyone other than Hilary as my wife.

God, I'd been so stupid.

And now I was paying the price.

Disgust twisted his mouth into a sneer. "Love has nothing to do with this! It's about *respect* and right now not only are you treating me with disrespect, you're treating your candidacy as a joke."

I stiffened. "You're right. The candidacy deserves more respect from me, but you, on the other hand, do not. You have to earn respect and I can't think of a single thing you've done to earn mine."

My father's reddened face darkened. "I'll be more lenient since you are obviously drunk, but I will remind you now, and then again when you're more sober, that there is *much more* at stake than your pride, Joseph."

I clenched my fists. "Just leave her out of this."

"You have to accept that there is no life for you with Rose Gardner. She's moving on without you and you need to do the same." He picked up his briefcase and set it on the chair next to me.

I turned to look out the window out into the parking lot. "I don't want to talk about Rose." That was a flat-out lie. I wanted to talk about Rose and ached to actually talk *to* her. How many times had I picked up my phone and almost called her? But I didn't want to talk about her with *him*.

He pulled a folder from his bag and held it toward me. "She's still working with that drug addict she hired and she's been spending a large amount of time with that televangelist. I believe they've begun a relationship."

"*Jonah Pruitt*?" I asked before I could stop myself. My gaze landed on the folder.

A hint of a grin lifted his mouth. "Yes, I believe that's his name. I have several photos of them embracing. She's been seen coming and going from his home and spending hours with him."

Anger surged in my chest, boiling my blood. "You've had her watched?" But beyond my irritation at his surveillance, anger that she'd already moved on, and who she'd moved on *with,* filled my head. I'd always presumed she'd end up with Mason. Was she upset and devastated enough to end up with that low-life Pruitt? His mother almost killed her and then he must have swooped in and took advantage of her vulnerable state. How could Mason let this happen? I wanted to drive to Henryetta and beat the shit out of both of them.

Just to drive his point home, Dad set the folder on the table and opened it, spreading photos of a woman with Jonah. I tried to look away, but my traitorous eyes refused. The two people in the photo were undeniably Rose and Jonah, and there was no doubt they were embracing. To prove his point, they were in different clothes in three set of photos. His investigator had caught them at least three times. Tears filled my eyes.

"I see that you're upset."

"And that's exactly why you did it." I shook my head, amazed that my father would stoop that low. But why was I surprised? Hadn't he proven he'd go to any lengths to get what he wanted?

"I did this to prove to you that *you need to let her go.*"

I twisted to face him. "What the hell? I haven't contacted her. I'm doing what you asked."

"No." My father glared his contempt. "You *haven't* been doing what I asked at all. You may be here on the campaign trail, but you aren't trying. Not since the first few days and now you're losing in the polls. Voters smell apathy a hundred yards away and you reek of it. Where's the enthusiasm you showed when you announced your candidacy?"

The first few days I'd been numb with grief over losing Rose. It had been so easy to slip into my familiar role—Joe Simmons, asshat charmer. And Hilary's presence had helped ease me into the persona. The press conference announcing my candidacy had gone well, too well when I took into account that Hilary had gotten carried away with her role as my fiancée, pulling me into a hug and an amorous kiss, and strategically placing her large-stoned engagement ring on my arm. We'd made headlines, even gotten attention on a national morning news show. We were big news and ahead in the polls right out of the gate.

However, I'd still been going through the motions for a few days after that, convincing myself that Rose's well-being depended on my performance. But I missed her more than I thought it was possible to miss another person. I couldn't eat, couldn't sleep, and Hilary's continual presence made me physically ill.

My fear for Rose had eased, and I'd let my performance slip. Why should I be surprised my father was here to remind me what I was really running for? Hurting me by pointing out that there was nothing to go back to with Rose was pure bonus.

I shoved the photos back in the folder then turned away. I couldn't face them.

"I need to go make a few phone calls. Make yourself a cup of coffee and get yourself together within the next two hours or there will be hell to pay." He stormed out of the room, leaving the incriminating folder on the table.

I picked up the folder to throw it in the trash but I needed to see her again, even if it was in Jonah's arms. Against what little sense I had left, I spread the photos on the table, searching for a photo of Rose alone. Most were of her with Jonah and Bruce Wayne, but I found one at the bottom of the stack. She'd been working outside and leaned on a shovel, looking at something out of view. She had on a pair of worn jeans and long-sleeved T-shirt, topped with a brown cardigan sweater. Her hair was pulled back and the wind had made her cheeks rosy. A hint of a smile lifted her mouth.

Gripping the photo with two hands, I lifted it closer to examine her left hand. Her fingers were bare, and a knot cramped my stomach. Why would I expect her to still be wearing my ring? She'd never even accepted my proposal, not to mention I was the one who left her. But I still held on to the dream that she believed I'd figure out a way to be with her. But that was completely illogical. I'd told her that we were done. No going back.

I shuffled through the photos with clumsy fingers and found several photos of Rose with Jonah, obviously taken the same day. In one they were facing each other as Rose gazed into Jonah's face, holding his hand. A second showed them sitting on a porch, their legs pressed together and Jonah leaning into her. In the third, they were standing and in a tight embrace, Rose's face buried in his chest.

I felt like I was strangling.

I heard a knock at the door but ignored it, sure it was my father coming back to gloat. Seconds later, Hilary entered the room and stopped next to me, taking in the photo in my hands.

"Joe," she said in a hushed tone. "Don't do this to yourself."

A lump formed in my throat, and I fought to take a breath.

She pried the photo from my hands and tossed it on the table. "Joe, you have to stop torturing yourself like this." Her voice was deceptively comforting.

I turned to her in my drunken haze, drowning in my agony. Rose had moved on without me.

With Jonah Pruitt.

Hilary reached a hand to my cheek, and stroked lightly before brushing my hair from my forehead. "Joe, you know your father will do anything to make sure you run in this race. Even resort to hurting you to keep you in line as evidenced by the photos on that table." Her eyes filled with tears. "Don't let him hurt you like this. Don't give him that power."

"I can't do this." My voice broke.

She pulled me into a hug. "Let me help you."

I clung to her, desperately wishing she was Rose.

"You don't have to do this alone, Joe." She leaned back to look into my eyes. "Let me *help* you."

I shook my head, confused. How could Hilary help me?

She looped her hands around my neck and pressed her body against mine.

I stiffened at the contact. I put my hands on her waist to push her away.

Her mouth hovered inches over my face. "Let me help you," she whispered huskily. Before I could answer, her lips touched mine.

I closed my eyes, feeling her tongue coax mine to respond. Weeks of pent-up sexual frustration erupted and my arms tightened around her back, pulling her closer as I kissed her back with an eagerness of my own.

*What was I doing?* I jerked backward, bumping into the bed. "*No!*"

She advanced toward me, her face soft and understanding. "Why are you holding back? Because of Rose? I know you're hurting right now and I want to help you. She's moved on, Joe, and so should you."

She was blurry through my tears. Had Rose really moved on without me? Wasn't that what I told her to do? I choked on a cry of agony.

"Joe." She pushed me until I sat on the edge of the bed and stood between my legs. "I can't stand to see you like this, baby. Let her go and let me help you." Her hand stroked my cheek and smoothed back the hair off my forehead. "You have to let her go."

"*I can't.*"

"*Why?*"

"I love her."

"I know you do, but she's moved on." She leaned into my face. "*I* love you, Joe. And I promise you that I won't leave you, even when you tell me to go away. If she really loved you, she would wait, just like I've done. My love is real, Joe. I know you better than anyone knows you. I'll be better this time. I promise. I'll be the girlfriend you need. Just let her go and give me another chance."

I shook my head.

She placed kisses on my cheeks, moving closer to my mouth. "You know you want this." She reached for my crotch. "And *I* know you want this. Don't fight it, Joe. *Just feel.*" She pushed me backward on the bed, straddling my hips as she leaned down and kissed me.

I closed my eyes, giving in to the feelings cascading through my body. I'd been numb for weeks and welcomed feeling something. Anything.

Hilary pulled off her shirt and tugged at my clothes, until I was naked. I kept my eyes closed, pretending it was Rose. Even in my drunken state, I knew I'd just sold my soul to the devil.

But my life was so hopeless, what did it matter?

# Rose

# Chapter Ten

*A day earlier*

The crisp wind blew strands of hair loose from my ponytail as I pressed the shovel into the dirt. It had been two weeks since Jonah's mother had tried to kill me, but my back still ached especially since I spent the day digging up bushes.

"It's looking good," Jonah Pruitt called out.

I looked over my shoulder and smiled. "It's getting there."

He stopped next to me, his left arm in a sling. He was recovering from his gunshot wound, but his spirits were still low. I imagined it would be hard to walk around in a good mood when you found out your mother had been killing women, reasoning that she was doing you a favor. "I'm just glad you didn't hold a grudge against me."

I leaned against the shovel. "We've been over this before. Why on earth would I hold a grudge? You were just as much a victim as I was."

"Well, thankfully, half the town has been as forgiving as you."

"And the other half?"

A wry smile lifted his mouth. "You really have to ask?"

No, but one could always hope that the narrow-minded citizens of Henryetta would have an epiphany. "Well, thanks for letting us still work on your yard. Bruce Wayne needs the work."

Jonah's eyes softened. "And maybe you do too."

I had visited Jonah in the hospital to make sure he was handling everything okay, and I'd ended up telling him all about Joe and the closest version of the truth that I'd told anyone about why we split. After he was discharged from the hospital, we'd gotten together for coffee a couple of times at his house. He was a good listener and not prone to giving unsolicited advice, unlike my sister.

Violet had insisted that I stay with her the first week, and I had to admit that it was easy to fall into the old habit of relying on her. But she wanted me to grieve according to her rules, and I'd begun to feel smothered. So Muffy and I went home, as hard as the loneliness was to face. Even with Joe's absence, home was familiar and comforting. Neely Kate had come over a couple of times with movies and ice cream, and we'd even had a slumber party one night, something I'd never had as a kid.

But the best thing I'd done to make myself feel better was to jump back into the landscaping portion of our business. Word had spread about the job we'd done at the New Living Hope Revival Church, and we'd gotten two other jobs in addition to Jonah's house, which we'd just started that morning.

I snuck a glance at Bruce Wayne. He was digging up an overgrown shrub and had nearly wrestled it free. I liked working, but I especially liked working with Bruce Wayne. He was great company. He was there if I needed him, but didn't talk much and didn't constantly ask if I was okay.

Just like Mason.

After Mason dropped me off at the nursery following my interview with Detective Taylor, he had called and texted a few times, letting me know that he was there for me if I needed him.

But otherwise, he'd kept his distance and I wasn't sure what to make of it.

"I'm glad you and Bruce Wayne have found each other," Jonah said, pulling me out of my thoughts.

"Yeah," I sighed. "Most people don't understand us. Especially Violet." She'd had a fit when she realized I was not only returning to work, but still working with Bruce Wayne. She said I had enough strikes against me, that associating with a known habitual criminal would be the final nail in my social coffin now that I was no longer dating a state policeman.

Jonah's mouth twisted in a grimace. "Violet has her own issues to work out, but she avoids them by focusing on other people's instead. I think you were smart to go back home."

My eyes widened in surprise.

"Forgive me if I'm speaking out of turn."

I shook my head. "No. You're only saying what I've already thought. Violet wants things to go back the way they were before I dated Joe and before—" I stopped myself from saying before Violet started having an affair, "—before Mike left her." I released a heavy sigh. "But I'm not the same person I was before Momma died. And I don't want to go back to being that person."

"And you shouldn't. That would be like asking Bruce Wayne to go back to being the man he was before he was accused of murder. Why would anyone want that?"

I nodded. He was right, but Violet was still unhappy with me. I'd always been her pet project until I didn't need her anymore. She'd seen my breakup with Joe as an opportunity to go back to the way things were before. Only I wasn't cooperating. "She loves me. She really does."

"Of course she does. No one's disputing that. But she's unhappy with her own life, Rose and she's transferring that unhappiness onto you. That's not fair."

A gust of wind blew several strands of hair into my face, and I pushed it over my ear. "You sound like a psychologist."

He smiled. "That's because I am one. Licensed even."

My mouth gaped. "I didn't know that."

"The license is under my old name. Before I changed my name from Jonas to Jonah. Which means I can't use it."

"Maybe you should quit hiding."

He sighed and shook his head. "Rose."

I looked up at him. "No, Jonah. You try so hard to make everyone else feel like they have a second chance. If you told them about your past, it would have so much more impact that they could change too."

"Rose," his voice lowered as he glanced at Bruce Wayne. "You of all people know how the people of this town would react if they found out about my criminal record." He grimaced. "Henryetta might not be heaven, but I'm tired of running."

"Exactly." I grabbed his hand. "So stop running."

He smiled but sadness filled his eyes. "I'll think about it."

As I watched the conflict on his face, I realized I needed to take my own advice. I was tired of running too. "I'd like to ask a favor."

"Of course."

I shook my head, grinning up at him. "You don't even know what it is yet."

"Honestly, I can't imagine you asking something of me that I'd refuse. After what my mother did—"

I grabbed his arm, my fingers digging through his dress shirt to get his attention. "Stop. You don't owe me anything, Jonah."

He remained silent.

"Don't say yes, just listen, okay?"

He nodded.

"I know you're not a licensed psychologist as Jonah, but you can still listen to someone as a friend, right?"

"Well…yeah."

"Mason suggested that I should talk to someone about everything I've been through the last few months, and I suspect he's right. The only problem is that I don't know who to talk to since all my troubles have something to do with my visions." I swallowed, suddenly nervous. "I was wondering if you would be willing to listen."

"Yes. Of course. But isn't that what we've already been doing?"

I took in a breath. He was right. We might not have called it therapy, but he'd been listening to me talk about my sorrows for two weeks. "But I haven't told you everything—like Daniel Crocker and the story of my birthmother."

"You were adopted?"

My chin trembled. "Not exactly, but it's a complicated story, and I haven't really dealt with it. Would you help me?"

His eyes glassed over. "I'd be honored."

"You were supposed to think about it before agreeing."

"Okay, let me think about it for a moment." His mouth lifted into a grin. "Yes, I accept."

Shaking my head, I laughed and gave him a hug, clinging to him. He truly had become a lifeline these past few weeks. "Thank you, Jonah. For everything."

His good arm tightened around me. "I'm not sure why you're thanking me."

"Because you've given me something I haven't had in a few weeks."

"And what's that?"

"Hope."

He leaned back and swallowed, struggling for an answer. Finally he gave me a lopsided grin. "Me too." He took a deep breath and released it. "How often would you like to meet? Weekly?"

"Or more often if you're willing."

His eyebrows lifted in surprise. "You're serious about this."

"I think Mason's right. I think I have a lot of issues to work through before I'm ready to move on."

"You mean with someone else?"

Tears filled my eyes.

"I heard about Joe and his old girlfriend."

Shock jolted my body. "What about them?"

Jonah looked horrified. "I'm sorry. I thought you knew."

My heart hammered in my chest. "I've purposely avoided the news. I didn't want any reminders of him, which included news about his campaign."

"Rose, I'm sorry."

"What is it? What do you know?"

His mouth pinched as indecision flooded his eyes.

"It's okay, Jonah. You can tell me." When he didn't respond, I added, "I had a vision before we broke up. I saw Joe married to Hilary. I knew they would get back together eventually."

Sadness filled his eyes. "I don't want to hurt you anymore than you already have been."

"Joe left *me*. He made it clear that we are done. I knew he'd move on, and it's no surprise he's with Hilary. It's what his family wants." I paused trying to catch my breath. I felt like I was drowning. "Now tell me what you know."

Jonah still looked uncertain. "When Joe announced his candidacy, he did it on the steps of the state capital with big media coverage. Hilary was at his side." He paused. "As his fiancée."

I took a step backward. "*Oh.*"

"I'm sorry."

I shook my head, but I was lightheaded and the movement made me stumble.

Jonah reached out and grabbed my elbow.

Bruce Wayne rose from the flower bed he was working on. "Miss Rose?"

I forced a smile. "I'm fine. I just tripped."

"Maybe you should sit down," Jonah suggested, leading me toward the front steps.

"I'm fine."

"Rose, if you're going to talk to me a couple of times a week about your past and your feelings, *now* is not the time to start lying to me."

Tears filled my eyes. "You're right. I'm sorry." I sat down on the front steps, Jonah sitting next to me. I shivered from the wind and the shock, and Jonah pressed his leg closer to mine.

"I know it's startling, even if you expected it."

Startling was an understatement. I felt numb. "The day after he broke up with me?" My voice quivered. "Are you sure?"

"Very sure. I was shocked after what you told me about him. But I have to say, he's getting slammed by the media. After their first couple of appearances, they haven't been very affectionate."

I sucked several deep breaths to try and clear my fuzzy head. I could see Joe pretending to be engaged to her, but they'd been affectionate. My heart was breaking all over again. "They were worried about him running against the other candidate as a single man. I guess they didn't waste any time."

He leaned toward, me, taking my hand. "I'm so sorry. I wish I hadn't told you."

"No." I shook my head, my voice firm as I looked into his eyes. "We're not together. He can do what he wants. I'm glad I know."

"Do you want to go home?"

Home to my empty house? Where memories of Joe permeated everything? "No, there's no reason to." I forced a smile. "I've got plenty to do here."

"Rose."

My jaw clenched. "Jonah, really. I need to work."

"Okay."

I spent the rest of the afternoon concentrating on nothing but the dirt and the plants. I knew that the fact I could block everything out so effectively wasn't normal, but it was a coping mechanism I'd learned early in life. It had helped me through more heartache than I thought I could endure, and I was especially thankful for the life skill now.

The overcast sky had threatened rain all day and by early afternoon it finally broke loose. Bruce Wayne and I waited in my truck for half an hour before we gave up and called it a day.

"The forecast is better for tomorrow," I said. "We'll just meet at eight again. With any luck at all, the rain will make it easier to dig out those overgrown shrubs."

"Sounds good, Miss Rose." Bruce Wayne stared out the front window, his jaw working. "If you need to take some time off, I can do this without you."

I knew this was his way of saying he understood what I was going through and wanted to help me. "I've taken more time off that I want. I need to work."

He nodded and opened the truck door. "I'll see you tomorrow."

As soon as Bruce Wayne climbed into his car and pulled away, I grabbed my cell phone out of my pocket and called Neely Kate.

"Rose, is everything okay?"

"He's engaged to Hilary," I said in a breathless rush.

"Oh no." There was a second pause. "How did you find out?"

"Jonah. He thought I knew."

"How could he get engaged to her so quickly? He just asked *you* to marry him a couple of weeks ago?" she growled.

I fought to keep from crying. "It's not a real engagement."

"How can you be sure? You know that witch has been waiting to get her claws back into him."

The devastation on Joe's face when I told him about my vision of him and Hilary still haunted me. "I know." But Jonah had said they were affectionate. I envisioned Hilary in the red dress she'd worn the night of Joe's parents' dinner and Joe in his tux. The image of Joe kissing her filled my head and I released a small gasp of anguish.

"I'm coming over tonight."

I'd been trying to become less dependent on her and everyone else, but I didn't want to be alone. "Okay."

"It's going to be okay, Rose. I promise."

I knew she was right, even if I didn't believe it right now.

I went home and took a bath then watched TV with Muffy, listening to the rain in my melancholy. I knew I had to tell Violet about Joe and decided to get it over with.

She listened then calmly asked, "Do you want to come spend the night with me?"

"Neely Kate's coming over." I paused. "Wait. Why don't you sound more surprised?"

When she didn't respond, the truth hit me. "You knew."

Her silence was damning.

"Why didn't you tell me?"

"I didn't want you to get hurt any more than you already were."

"Violet, I had a right to know."

"I know you did. I'm sorry." Her voice softened. "You've just been through so much, you needed a break. I wanted to protect you."

"I'm not eight years old anymore, Violet. You can't protect me from life."

She was silent for several seconds. "You'll always be my little sister, Rose. Neither one of us can change that. I love you. I'll always want to protect you."

I knew she meant well, but this was one more sign of her smothering.

"Are you sure you don't want to come spend the night?"

"No." Even if I'd been tempted before—and I wasn't—I definitely didn't want to go now.

"How'd it go at Jonah's today?"

I sighed. Back to a somewhat safe topic. "We got a lot of work done today before the rain hit."

"Are you sure you're ready to be doing all the manual labor? You're still recovering."

"My back hurts some, so I'm a lot slower than Bruce Wayne, but I like being there. You know that working in the dirt makes me feel better."

"Okay. I just don't want you to overdo it."

"I'm fine."

"Someone stopped in and asked about another landscaping job. Will you be in the shop tomorrow morning? I'll give you the address and the phone number so you can set up an appointment."

"Wow. Another? That's great."

"We're really doing well," she said, breathless with excitement. "We've already gotten landscaping jobs and business here at the nursery is picking up now that cooler weather has set in."

"Look at the Gardner sisters," I said. "Lucky in business. Unlucky in love."

"Rose," Violet's voice was heavy with sorrow.

"I'm okay," I said, sorry for my moment of wallowing and sorry for making her remember her own heartache. "This is a good thing. Really. Joe has moved on and so will I. It'll all work out in the end."

"Yes, it will. I have to believe that. For both of us."

I knew she wasn't talking about just me and Joe. Neely Kate walked in the side door carrying a bag. She stopped and put two containers in the freezer.

"Neely Kate's here. I have to go. I'm meeting Bruce Wayne at Jonah's at eight tomorrow. I'll come by probably mid-morning to pick up the landscaping bricks and get the information about the new landscape job."

"Okay, I'll see you tomorrow." She paused. "I love you, Rose."

"Love you too." And I did. In spite of her shortcomings. Lord knew I wasn't perfect.

Neely Kate set the bag on my coffee table and shrugged out of her jacket.

"Is it romantic comedies or action movies tonight?" I asked, leaning over to look in her bag.

She jerked it away from me with a laugh. "Neither. It's time to step up your game since you've missed most major television events of the past decade."

"So what is it?"

"*Grey's Anatomy*. Nothing like Doctors McDreamy and McSteamy to cheer you up." She set the DVD case on the table, then pulled out a Tupperware container. "And my grandma's homemade potato soup. She heard about Joe and Hilary and whipped up a batch just for you."

"She knows about Joe and Hilary?"

Neely Kate shrugged. "I was supposed to take her to get hot wings and then to the VFW bingo night."

"I'm sorry."

She rolled her eyes and put a hand on her hip. "Girl. Please. You saved me. Have you ever *been* to bingo night at the VFW?"

"No."

"Well, don't do it. Just *don't*." She went into the kitchen. "So when I told her about Joe, she let me off the hook and made you soup." She had two bowls and spoons when she reemerged. "You obviously did me a huge favor. All the way around. I love her potato soup."

"What about Ronnie?"

She sat down and lifted the lid off the plastic container. "He's got poker night with the guys at the garage, which is how I got roped into bingo night. I'd much rather be with you eating soup and Ben and Jerry's."

"You brought Ben and Jerry's?"

Her eyes widened in dismay. "What kind of friend do you take me for? *Of course* there's Ben and Jerry's."

I leaned over and gave her a sideways hug. "You're the best friend I could ever have."

She hugged me back then pulled away and rolled her eyes. "Well that goes without saying. I'm introducing you to the *many* hot men of Seattle Grace Hospital." She tilted her head to the side with a smirk. "You're welcome."

She started the first episode and we snuggled under afghans as the rain pounded the roof. After the second episode, she paused the DVD and grabbed the ice cream from the freezer, holding up two containers. "Here we have Cherry Garcia, my personal favorite, and then Phish Food, because I know how much you like chocolate." She put the containers on the table, ripped off the lids and handed me the Phish Food container.

I took it and the clean spoon she offered. "No bowls?"

She shrugged, leaning back with her own ice cream. "What's the point of dirtying bowls? Especially when you don't have a dishwasher."

I dug my spoon into the ice cream. "True."

"So what do you think?" she asked, studying the ice cream on her spoon.

"I like it. Momma never let me watch *Grey's Anatomy* because she said a show about doctors fornicating in hospital hallways was the devil's handiwork."

"Your momma sure made the devil out to be one busy guy."

I laughed. "Yeah. She did."

"But I wasn't talking about the show. I meant Joe." She twisted her head to look at me.

"What's there to think about?"

"Do you think he's really with her or is it a political move? I looked up some articles online and the reporters suspect they're not really together. They were touchy feeling the first few days, but the articles pointed out that Hilary initiated all of it."

I dug my spoon deep into the ice cream with more force than necessary. "What difference does it make? Joe broke up with me. He can marry whoever he likes."

"He still loves you, Rose."

My gaze rose to her face. "It doesn't matter, Neely Kate. We are *done*. We *all* need to accept that. Even you."

"But Rose—"

"Did you know Jonah used to be a psychologist? He used to counsel people."

Her face scrunched in confusion. "I guess that's not so surprising. He's a minister. They help people."

"I asked him if I could talk to him a couple of times a week."

Her spoon lowered over her container as her mouth gaped. "You did?"

I glanced down at my container. "Before Joe broke up with me, Mason told me that I couldn't keep shoving everything under the rug. That I have to face my past and everything bad that's happened." I looked up at her. "I think he's right. I'm ready to do it. I *need* to do it so I can move on too."

"You really want to do this?"

I nodded, tears filling my eyes. "I asked Jonah, before I knew about Joe and Hilary, but hearing the news was the confirmation I needed that it's time to quit wallowing. It's time to pick myself up, dust myself off, and keep going. I'm tired of being weak. I'm tired of falling to pieces whenever I hear his name."

"Rose, it's okay to wallow a little. That doesn't make you weak."

"But happiness is a choice, Neely Kate. I could get stuck in this pit of feeling sorry for myself, but I don't want to. I don't like it here. I want to climb out and I want to live my life." I leaned closer to her. "I want to be *happy*. I had a taste of it with Joe and I want to feel it again. Even if it seems impossible to feel it without him."

She put her ice cream on the table and took my hand. "No one deserves happiness more than you do. You *will* be happy. I promise."

"And when I sort out the mess of my life, then I'll be ready to try being with someone else. I need to sort me out first."

A soft smile lifted the corners of her mouth but her eyes filled with tears. "You've just said the smartest thing I've heard in ages."

I blinked back tears. "Thanks."

"And you *do* know someone is waiting for you to be ready don't you?"

I nodded, a blush rising to my cheeks. "Yeah. I suspect he is."

"Have you seen him?"

"Not since the day I gave my statement to the police. But he calls every so often and he texts me telling me that he's there for me if I need him."

"I always said Mason Deveraux was a smart man."

I laughed and scooped out a spoonful of ice cream. "No, I think you said he had a corn cob stuck up his butt."

She giggled and stuck her spoon in my ice cream. "Well, at the time he *did*." She winked. "He just needed a woman to soften him up."

I shook my head with a grin.

"But if he's not interested, Austin Kent, Violet's friend is still available. The guy she set you up with at her impromptu barbeque, remember him?"

My brow lowered with a scowl. "How do you know he's available?"

She shrugged. "I knew he was interested before and I did some checking. So see? You have options. And the fact you're considering them is a good thing."

She started the next episode and I tried to concentrate on the latest Seattle Grace disaster, but I keep thinking about being with another man. It felt weird and wrong.

Could I really consider finding love again? Would I ever really be over Joe?

# Chapter Eleven

Several days later, Bruce Wayne and I finished Jonah's yard. We stood back at the curb, taking it all in. All the overgrown shrubbery had been removed, and we'd put in new bushes, along with a mix of chrysanthemums and perennials. We'd built a foot-tall retaining wall on the side of the house with landscaping blocks, dug up the crumbling sidewalk from the driveway to the front porch, and laid a brick paver path. We'd worked hard all week and it had paid off. The front of the house looked beautiful.

"We did a good job, Miss Rose."

I grinned, feeling real happiness for the first time in weeks. "Yes, we did. We need to celebrate."

He turned to me in surprise.

"I'm taking you out to lunch."

His head ducked and his face reddened. "You don't have to do that."

"I know, but I want to. I *need* to celebrate something, Bruce Wayne."

His face lifted and he nodded, understanding in his eyes. "Sounds good."

We loaded up the remaining tools in the back of my truck and washed our hands in the spigot at the side of Jonah's house. He was going to be thrilled at the transformation. I was sorry he wasn't here to see it.

Bruce Wayne headed for his car.

"Hold up a minute," I called after him, pulling my phone out of my pocket. I pulled up Jonah's number and called him. He needed something happy in his life too even if it was something as simple as his house looking pretty.

"Hey, Rose." He greeted me with warmth in his voice. "I was just thinking about you and Bruce Wayne. How's it coming?"

I grinned, knowing he couldn't see it, but I couldn't keep my joy to myself. "We're done."

"You are?"

"Want to come see?"

"Yeah." He sounded happier than I had ever heard him. "I'll be right there."

Fifteen minutes later, Jonah pulled into his driveway. His face lit up with a smile as he got out of his car. "Rose, Bruce Wayne...It's wonderful!"

I looped my arm through his right arm. "It looks a lot more welcoming now."

He shook his head in amazement. "I'm glad I tried not to look at it the last couple of days. It looks so much more impressive this way." He glanced down at me. "I know it must look silly to be so excited over something like landscaping..." His voice trailed off. "It feels like home now. Like I belong here."

"Jonah," I leaned close and lowered my voice. "You know that I, of all people, get it. That's why I called you."

His eyes softened. "Thanks."

"We're both making progress, a few steps at a time."

He nodded. "I just wish everyone was as forgiving as you are."

"Maybe they'll get there, but until then, you've got me. And Bruce Wayne." I gasped. "Hey! We were just going to go eat lunch and celebrate. Why don't you come with us?"

"Oh." Some of his excitement faded. "I don't want to encroach."

"We'd really like if you came," I said, tugging on his arm. "Wouldn't we, Bruce Wayne?"

He nodded, looking Jonah in the eyes. "Yes, sir. We would."

"Besides," I said, squeezing his arm. "You're the reason we're celebrating. We have two landscape jobs lined up after this and possibly a third, and all thanks to you. It was the work on your church and house that got us the new jobs. So you *have* to come. It wouldn't be the same without you."

He smiled. "Well, okay then."

"Good. It's settled. Where do you two want to go?"

Bruce Wayne and Jonah picked Merilee's café, so I called Neely Kate on the way and invited her to meet us in ten minutes.

"I love that you're celebrating something," she squealed. "I wouldn't dream of missing it."

I parked half-block away. Bruce Wayne and Jonah were waiting at the entrance to the restaurant along with Neely Kate.

Her face lit up with a smile when I reached her. "Thanks for letting me crash your celebration."

I gave her a huge hug. "I wouldn't dream of celebrating without you."

Neely Kate opened the door and held it open. "They're already setting up a table for us so go on in."

Neely Kate patted Bruce Wayne's arm as he grabbed the door and motioned for us to walk in. A waitress motioned us to the back where she had pushed two tables together.

"Rose, you sit at the end of the table," Neely Kate said.

I counted our group, wondering if I'd gotten the number wrong. "Why do we need two tables? There's only four of us and we'll all fit at one."

She shrugged with a grin. "I hope you don't mind if I invited someone to join us."

"Of course not." Had she called Violet? I hoped not. I felt some guilt not including her, but the people at this lunch had done everything in their power to build me up, not tear me down. The fact I couldn't include Violet in the bunch was telling enough.

"Good." Neely Kate tilted her head toward the front door. "He's walking across the street now."

The front door opened and Mason filled the doorway. His gaze swept the room and landed on me, his face lighting up.

"It just seemed like he needed to be here," she said, glancing back at him and then me.

A soft smile lifted my mouth and my chest tightened. "Yeah, it's perfect now."

Mason moved to the end of the table and hesitated. "I hope you don't mind that Neely Kate invited me. Is it okay if I join you?"

I nodded, trying to keep from tearing up. I wasn't sure why I was so happy he was here, but I realized I was celebrating with my friends, which meant he belonged here too.

His smile spread across his face as he extended a hand toward Bruce Wayne. The two men shook and Mason looked Bruce Wayne in the eyes, congratulating him on helping to make the Gardner Sisters Nursery a success. The respect he showed Bruce Wayne filled my heart with an unexpected warmth.

Bruce Wayne's gaze lowered. "It's all Miss Rose. She comes up with the ideas. I just do the diggin' and plantin'."

I shook my head with a laugh. "Don't let him fool you. I couldn't do it without him. We're a team."

Mason nodded, pride in his eyes as he glanced at me. "I believe that's probably true."

We all sat down, me at one end and Mason at the other, with Neely Kate and the other two men on the sides. We ordered lunch and talked about our landscaping jobs then Jonah's decreased church attendance.

"But the members who have stayed seem even more committed than before," Jonah said, absently poking his fork as his salad.

"You'll build it back up," Neely Kate reached over and patted his hand. "And your church will be stronger for it. Especially since you seem more genuine now. No offense, Jonah, but you were kind of creepy and overbearing before."

"Neely Kate!" I gasped.

Jonah lifted his hands in surrender, wincing when he lifted his left arm too high. "No, it's true, Rose. I've listened to my mother's advice and suggestions for over two years, but now I just want to be myself. It's going to take some time to figure out who that is." His gaze found mine and he smiled softly. "Just like you're trying to figure out who *you* are now."

Confusion flickered in Mason's eyes, but he remained silent.

We spent the next forty minutes telling stories and laughing. I was surrounded by people who cared about me and I cared about them. Joe had called them outcasts, and he was probably right. Even Mason had been cast out of Little Rock as penance for his crime, but I was an outcast too. *These people* were who I belonged with. A warm happiness flooded my chest, and I felt like there was nothing too daunting for me to tackle.

I cast a glance at Mason and found him watching me with a soft smile. We locked eyes and my stomach fluttered before I looked away.

When we finished lunch, I hugged each one of my friends goodbye, but I saved Mason for last. We stood alone on the sidewalk outside the café, neither one of us speaking. The crisp late October wind gently blew my hair into my eyes as I stared up into Mason's face, my hands stuffed into my jean pockets.

"Are you cold?" he asked, starting to remove his jacket.

"No," I said with a smile. "I'm fine."

"You look good, Rose," he said, softly. "You look happy."

I shifted my feet. "I'm getting there." I paused. "I took your advice."

Confusion wrinkled his brow. "What advice?"

"You told me I had to face what I've been through. That I have to work through it to move on. You were right, and I've been doing that."

He released a breath, his warm eyes glittering. "Good. I'm glad."

"Jonah was a licensed therapist in Texas, so we get together twice a week now and talk about... things." I bit my lower lip before continuing. "I need to figure out who I am alone before I can figure out who I am with someone else." I tilted my head. "Does that make sense?"

He smiled, looking relieved. "It makes perfect sense."

I knew he'd understand. He'd been there for me through so much, but I didn't realize how much I liked having him around until that moment. His absence the last couple of weeks had left a hole in my life. I took a step closer. "I miss you, Mason."

Indecision flickered in his eyes before he rested his hand on my upper arm. "I miss you too." He cleared his throat. "But I needed to give you some time to get over Joe. I hope you don't think I deserted you. I just...I wanted..."

His voice trailed off, and I laughed. "Why Mason Deveraux, I don't know that I've ever seen you at a loss for words."

He chuckled, glancing at the courthouse across the street then back at me. "It's a pretty rare occurrence. It takes something extraordinary to make that happen."

"This conversation is extraordinary?"

He hesitated, his smile fading slightly. "No, I'm calling *you* extraordinary."

"Oh." My heart sped up.

Indecision warred on his face again before resolve squared his jaw. "I care about you, Rose. I'm sure I haven't done a very good job of hiding my feelings. Even when you were with Joe. But I never would have interfered when you were with Joe. I care about you too much to have put you in that position. Now he's out of the picture, but I didn't want you to rush into something you weren't ready for. I wanted to give you space to sort through your feelings over your breakup."

I looked into his eyes, worried. "Mason, I... Joe was my first boyfriend. I loved him. I still do."

The pain that flickered in his eyes sent a stab of pain through my stomach.

"But he and I are over. I know that. I just need to adjust before I can move on."

Relief washed over his face and he nodded. "I know and I want to respect that."

"I've also done a lot of growing and changing myself over the last five months and as Jonah has pointed out, a lot of it has been with Joe. I need to figure out who I am now that I'm not under Momma's iron fist and no longer in a relationship with Joe. I need to figure out who Rose Gardner of Henryetta, Arkansas is on my own before I can figure out who I am with someone else."

"I understand." Thankfully, he looked like he really did.

"I'm not sure what I feel for you Mason, but I know I like you. A lot. And I miss you so much it hurts." I looked down at his red tie, suddenly embarrassed at my confession.

He reached under my chin and tilted my face up to meet his gaze. "I know that I like you too. A lot."

I smiled.

"I miss you too. You have no idea how hard it is for me, but I'm willing to until you're ready. I think we could have something really amazing, but I want you to be sure. With no regrets and no hesitation."

"Thank you for understanding."

His face lowered to mine and my breath caught as I wondered if he was going to kiss me, but his lips brushed my cheek. "You're worth waiting for."

I threw my arms around his neck, burying my face into his chest, unwilling to let him go yet. His arms tightened around me, and we embraced for several seconds, the wind lifting the edges of my coat, giving me a chill. The way my heart sped up when he held me in his arms, I wondered what else we could have between us. Part of me wanted to be with him now and I considered telling him that I didn't want to wait. But that wouldn't be fair to him and it wouldn't be fair it me either.

Because I knew I wasn't ready yet.

I released my hold on his neck, sliding my hands down to his chest, still unable to step away. Mason's arms still encircled my back, and he dipped his head to leave a lingering kiss on my forehead. I tilted my face up to look into his, surprised at the intensity of his gaze.

"I need to let you go before I do something I'll regret." His arms dropped and he took a half-step away. "I have no right making any demands on you, and I won't. I'll let you set the pace."

"But you want it to be soon?" I whispered.

His hand reached for my face, his thumb stroking my cheek. "Thank you for waiting."

Emotion flickered in his eyes. "How could I not?" Then he dropped his hold on me. "I'm always here when you need me, Rose." Then he turned and crossed the street toward the courthouse.

I watched him stop at the entrance and open the door, his gaze landing on me one last time before he disappeared inside. Instead of feeling lonely and empty because of his absence, I basked in the hope that maybe I really could be happy again with someone else. Mason was right. When I started a new relationship, I wanted to do it with no regrets.

I just needed to give myself time.

*Thirty-One and a Half Regrets* coming January 9, 2014

# About the Author

New York Times and USA Today bestselling author Denise Grover Swank was born in Kansas City, Missouri and lived in the area until she was nineteen. Then she became a nomadic gypsy, living in five cities, four states and ten houses over the course of ten years before she moved back to her roots. She speaks English and smattering of Spanish and Chinese which she learned through an intensive Nick Jr. immersion period. Her hobbies include witty Facebook comments (in own her mind) and dancing in her kitchen with her children. (Quite badly if you believe her offspring.) Hidden talents include the gift of justification and the ability to drink massive amounts of caffeine and still fall asleep within two minutes. Her lack of the sense of smell allows her to perform many unspeakable tasks. She has six children and hasn't lost her sanity. Or so she leads you to believe.

You can find out more about Denise and her other books at:
www.denisegroverswank.com
or email her at denisegroverswank@gmail.com

CPSIA information can be obtained at www.ICGtesting.com
Printed in the USA
LVOW10s1805081215

465959LV00025B/1668/P